I can do all things through Christ who strengthens me.
Philippians 4:13

Other books by Rosalyn Stowell
Don't Use A Chainsaw In The Kitchen – How-to and Cookbook
PAW (Post Apocalyptic World) Trilogy
The Beginning – Book 1
The Dark of Night – Book 2
The Dawn – Book 3
Alaskan Gold – novel, romance
Alaskan Alibi – novel, suspense
Stikine – novel, suspense
Cold Gold – novel, suspense
Klondike – novel, historical
A Head Of The Game – novel, serial killer
A Rat by Any Other Name….SHTF novel
Trouble in Paradise –a Paradise, Alaska novel

A Rat by Any Other Name...
An Alaskan SHTF Novel
By
Rosalyn Stowell

Chapter 1

The young woman felt fear so deep she thought she was having a heart attack. She knew someone may have spotted her making one last trip to her home, trying to salvage as much stuff as she possibly could. She was also very angry. How could their own government have come to this? She was always telling everyone they were over reacting to the threat from Washington D.C. and now she knew just how wrong she had been. Would she survive to ever tell anyone and would there be anyone left to tell? Who knew? What a mess.

Here it was, the end of July. With no snow it was difficult to pull her loaded akio sled along but it was the only way she could manage to take enough supplies to possibly survive. This was her fourth trip and she knew she would not get another.

The sounds coming up the road let her know she was cutting it fine as it was. Once in a while, sporadic gunfire let her know the advancing patrol thought they saw someone or something out in the trees. They were shooting and asking questions later. She pitied any random moose they saw.

She was trying not to leave a trail and hoped they would not have tracking dogs with them. They would not be looking for her exactly, they were just looking for anyone that had not voluntarily turned themselves in. That made her suspect in their view and she would be fair game if anyone saw her.

As she trudged along, the tow strap gouging into her shoulder each time the akio snagged on a stick or rock, she reviewed what she had heard early this morning. Could it only be less than 24 hours since her whole world had fallen apart?

She was in the yard cutting lengths of firewood when the old truck had careened into her yard and the old man that lived farther up the road was gasping when he stopped the truck.

"Are you okay? Do I need to drive you in to the hospital?" she had asked.

"No, if you take me in, neither one of us will make it back out from town. They are doing it. They are rounding everyone up and moving them to the camps we been hearing about."

"What are you talking about? Who is?"

"The fellas wearing blue helmets that our government has brought in as 'Peacekeepers' except they are the ones using guns." The old man wheezed.

"That can't be right. Why would they do that?"

"Well, missy, you just keep thinking it isn't happening and in a day or two, you can join the rest being herded into trucks and hauled away. They already shot Rich, here."

Then she had finally noticed the man slid down in the seat beside Travis. His face was pale and his hand pressed a rag against his shoulder where blood seeped out between his fingers.

"Bring him in the house and I will patch him up until you can get him back to a doctor." She said.

The old man glared at her, "You ain't listening, if we go back, we are both dead. They just shoot the old folks, not wasting space hauling an old person somewhere and feeding out good food for someone they can't retrain or work." He put the truck in reverse and was turned around and heading back before she could say anything else.

She wasn't sure what to think, so put up the saw and went in the house to check the radio. Sure enough, every station had the same message.

"This is an emergency. For your own safety, go to your nearest public shelter to be assigned a space on one of the relocation shuttles. Anyone not complying will be shot as looters."

Over and over the message played. She could not fathom how it had come to this. This was America.

Then panic set in and she rushed around the house, trying to grab everything she could carry and rushing out to her pickup. Yeah, right, where would she go, once everything was in the pickup? Besides, there are few roads in the State and they would already be blocked from heading south and went nowhere heading north or west. Then she considered that this pickup was fairly new and might have a GPS location system in it and left all the stuff she could do without in it. She repacked the old snowplow pickup with all the heaviest things she had, chainsaws, polydrums of gas and some kerosene, propane and oil. She managed to load some large pieces of membrane roofing and all the stovepipe, nails and assorted hand tools into the load, along with reloading and canning supplies.

When there was barely room for her to get into the driver's seat, she finally climbed in and eased the truck down the hill, between trees where there was no road or trail. She had her two cats in a pet carrier stuffed onto the dash on the passenger side and all the food and litter she had on hand in with the load of her own stuff in the cab.

She would not abandon her only companions and they would help her be alert to intruders and vermin control.

Once she had the truck as far down the hill as she could easily manage, she locked it, covered the whole thing with a brown tarp, leaving a window slightly open for ventilation for the cats. Then she trudged back up the hill to see what she could manage to bring along, dragging on the akio.

Now she had 4 loads counting the one she was dragging, stashed down near the truck. She tried using a slightly different route each trip so no really good trail would show to anyone looking for her. An experienced tracker could find her in a heartbeat, but she was hoping the people headed this way were town folk, not used to country living and hunting.

Once she made it to her truck, she uncovered it and began working her way farther around the hill. She would continue dragging her other supplies along, using the sled, when she parked the truck again and covered it.

The loads for the sled felt heavier each time she repacked and moved them and she was just about totally worn out when she came around a tree and ran straight into something solid and warm that grabbed or attempted to grab her.

Suddenly she found new energy to spare as she dropped her harness and took off. She hadn't done all this work just to give in easily. She wasn't going as fast as she thought she was though and soon a hand closed over her shoulder and spun her around. She used the momentum to punch whomever had a grip on her. She knew from the startled "Oof" that she had scored a fairly good blow and the hand released her shoulder. She took off again.

This time she was brought down with a tackle. Whomever was catching her actually had not used excessive force so far and even when tackling her, she managed not to be the one hitting the ground all that hard.

The irritating factor was that he not only managed to catch and tackle her, but had somehow also brought her sled along as he ran after her. She sat on the ground, puffing for air while the figure in coveralls lay on his back, hand to his head, puffing to draw air into the lungs she had jammed her elbows into as they fell.

"Okay, you caught me, now what?" she snarled.

"I was going to ask if I could help. I also wanted to know if you knew what is going on." He gasped. "I was walking to the store when I saw some vehicles pull in and a truck with a covered back. Men jumped out and were carrying guns. They went into the store, herded everyone out and then shot most of them. The few not shot were loaded into the back of the truck. What is happening?"

"Do you know Travis?"

"Yes, he gave me a hand when I first moved out here, a very nice man."

"Well, he stopped by a little bit ago on his way home from town and said everyone is being rounded up for relocation and all the elderly and infirm are being shot."

"How can this be happening? I knew some oddballs have been claiming this was going to happen, but how can it really happen here?" he appeared almost in shock.

"I don't know, but it is the same message on all the radio stations, to come turn yourself in and anyone not coming in will be shot as looters."

"I thought you had a newer pickup?"

"I do but saw no reason to use something with a GPS locator in it and be found that way, if anyone goes to that much trouble." She replied.

"Oh, good thinking. Do you want to go back for anything else?"

"I would love to, but the sounds of vehicles were coming up the hill near my driveway when I took off with this last load and I don't want to be caught that way, either. I was afraid to try bringing the 4 wheeler as it has a noisy motor and I didn't know how soon they would show up. The pickup is a lot quieter."

"Maybe we can check it out in a couple of days and see if it is safe to go back for anything you might want to save."

"I think it would be safer to stay away from any place they expect folks to come back to. I don't know if they would booby-trap or set traps for people, but they sound ruthless. I don't think anything left at the house is worth dying over."

They were talking in low tones, not whispering, as a whisper will usually carry farther than a low voice and sounds carry uphill very well. Now they proceeded on down to her pickup.

"How the devil did you get that down here?" he asked.

"It hasn't been easy. Right now, I think this is as far as I want to move it, so the sound of the motor doesn't give it away. I'm hoping no one will be stationed out here to keep an eye on the area."

"I wonder if they will patrol, once they have swept the area?"

"I wish I had paid more attention to the people that said this was going to happen. Maybe I could have made stashes out and about better than what I have managed today."

"I don't have anything stored away from my home, but my home isn't easily found, either. So far, not even hunters have stumbled across it."

She looked at him closer and did remember having seen him walking along the road once in a while.

"So you are living out here full time now?" she asked.

"Yes, once my property was paid for, I quit my job in town and moved out. I love the peace and quiet out here. By the way, my name is Gabe."

"Lynn." And they shook hands.

The sound of an explosion rent the air and they looked at each other in stunned surprise.

"That sounded over near the pipeline. Why would they demolish the capability of transporting oil from up north?" he asked.

"Was it their side or ours, doing the blowing? Maybe someone didn't want to let them step in and take over a working money making setup. Given a choice, I would make it as hard for them to take over as possible."

They looked at each other a minute, then dropped their loads, picked up weapons and started back up the hill. They would not go to her house, but angle down the hill toward the store.

They came into the yard from the back, slowly and carefully. The sight that met their eyes horrified and repelled them.

One man remained on a heavily armed vehicle while two others desecrated the dead. She motioned that she would get the one in the vehicle if he would take out the other two.

He wasn't sure what she had in mind but she melted away into the shadows before he could question how she planned on doing that.

He waited the 5 minutes she had hissed as she left, then worked his way down to the closest person. He never saw the man sitting behind the gun disappear, but suddenly she was sitting there and aiming the weapon at one of the men in front of him.

He slit the throat of the closest one and as the other turned, he clubbed him over the head. They loaded all the bodies on the back and the live one was bound firmly, including his mouth as they drove down toward the river.

"I wish we could give these folks a decent burial, but I would rather dump them in the river than allow anything happening like what we just saw." Lynn said.

He agreed. To him, these 'peacekeepers' were less than animals. If an animal kills, it is usually only for food. They do not amuse themselves by gross acts on the dead after they are done killing them.

They pulled the vehicle off the main road near the bridge and dumped the bodies over the side. Then followed an old trapping trail into the brush as far as they could manage with the vehicle. They unloaded all the weapons they found and placed them aside plus the uniforms they removed from the dead invaders. The live one was awake now and very uncooperative. She nudged him with her knife and he stopped struggling.

They placed the dead men in the seats and poured the can of gas from the back over the vehicle, then torched it. Then they loaded up themselves and their prisoner and started walking up the valley.

Any time they heard engines, they ducked under trees and brush and stayed still until they couldn't hear the sounds any more. The first time, the prisoner tried to resist, but he now sported another large knot on his head, and was more amenable to behaving.

Chapter 2

"I didn't realize how far down the valley we came with that vehicle. Too bad it would have a GPS system in it. We could have used it sometime."

"I'm just happy to add the weapons to our supplies. They are a little different than what I am familiar with, but I know how to use them." He replied.

They hiked on a bit farther when she asked him just what were they going to do with their extra mouth to feed?

"I'm not sure, but maybe we can get some answers out of him. I'm positive he speaks or understands English the way he reacts when we talk. I do speak a couple of the languages from the Near East."

"Okay, but I hate to waste good food on excess hateful baggage."

"Oh, he will earn his food. My wife will see to that."

"How is she going to take you showing up with two extras in tow?"

"She will welcome you. Him? Not so much."

She worried all the way to his home. Her first impression of his wife was that she had never seen such a beautiful exotic woman and why was she living out here in the middle of nowhere? She was exquisite.

The woman smiled shyly at her and offered her hand in welcome, "Hi, I'm Halya."

Before she could answer, the woman spotted the man behind her and reached behind her for a wicked looking knife, screamed something better left uninterpreted and lunged for the man.

Her husband caught her in mid jump and held her close, murmuring in her ear. Slowly she lowered the knife and the man behind them had a look of fear that made bringing him along worth it.

Halya spat some more words at him that he understood and he turned pale. He looked to the other two for protection from this small dainty looking woman intent on giving him a slow painful death.

Halya turned toward the door that appeared to open right into the hillside and motioned them inside.

"Where are my manners, you must be thirsty after that long walk." And she walked right on in to the house.

What a house it was. Inside, it was comfortable and roomy. Outside, it blended right into the hillside. "Wow, this is so fantastic. How did you manage to build all of this clear up in here without a road in?" Lynn asked.

"We brought most of the supplies in during the winter when we could drive up the trap line trail. We walked an old backhoe in, the same way. It is under cover out back in its own hillside garage. We preferred keeping low profile."

"I can understand that. Most of the people out here just want privacy and to be left alone. That is the main attraction to living out here. Not having to be social unless you want to be. I better be going and get my cats settled in for the night somewhere. I do thank you for the help today."

"Where do you plan on staying or is that none of my business? I did just sort of barge right in without permission." He smiled.

"Other than blind panic, I didn't really have a plan when I left the house today."

Halya was tugging on Gabe's sleeve by this time, then looked over at her with a smile on her face.

"Why not stay here? You can use the garage for your own privacy and then we can build you your own place similar to ours, if you like?"

Gabe smiled approval and she thought about it maybe 3 seconds before accepting. It would be safer for all of them to have extra eyes as lookouts and extra hands to work.

They unloaded all the spare equipment and gear taken from the burned vehicle and other troops from the prisoner and themselves, then started out to her stash of supplies.

When Halya saw how much she had managed to drag down the hill along with the pickup, she was amazed. They made up a load for the prisoner and he refused to carry it. Halya smiled and started for him and he not only picked it up, but started back to their house with it and as much else as he could pick up.

Lynn retrieved the pet carrier from the passenger seat of the pickup and a bag of food. The pans and bucket of litter all fit on the akio with room for her bedroll and a few other items. The cats were too scared to make noise, so they proceeded on down the valley to the garage.

The garage was as well-hidden as the house was. When the wide double doors swung open, she could hardly believe what she was seeing. There was a lot of room around the backhoe and if she could manage to bring the pickup this far, it would fit in here very well. No crowding.

Halya showed her where the outhouse was located and they left her to make a space her home for the time being while they went back to the house.

There were shafts of white PVC pipe located around the large room, letting in plenty of light as long as it was light outdoors. This time of year, that was not a problem, it was light 24/7

She did not want to move any of his tools or equipment around, so picked the side closest to the door where there was an empty work bench. Soon she had the cat's litter box and food dishes set out and her bed made over near the wall, then she let the cats out and sat on her bed, petting and crooning to them, trying to ease their ruffled feelings.

Soon there was a knock at the small side door she had not noticed earlier. Then Halya stepped in and smiled. "Is everything okay? I have dinner ready if you would please come eat with us?"

"This is wonderful. I am so happy to meet you and your husband both. I just wish it had been under different circumstances. Yes, I would love to share dinner with you." Lynn grabbed a small box she had stuck in her pack from the front seat of the truck on their way down to the house. "Here is a little something you might enjoy, later."

Halya peeked in the bag and smiled as she saw the box of chocolate truffles. "Oh yes, very much so, thanks."

As they ate, Gabe told her what he had found out so far from the prisoner. The President called in the UN to subdue and disarm the unruly population of Alaska. Alaska was being listed as a rogue State and no one was expected to comply with the new Law banning guns in private ownership. The prisoner said that since they were all infidels anyway, it gave them a chance to pave their way to Paradise. He considered Halya worse than an infidel, she was married to one of them and knew better. She should be stoned, then burned.

Gabe warned both of them to be extremely careful if they had to deal with the prisoner at all. They did not dare turn him loose.

Gabe thought Alaska was just being used to see how the other States reacted. If there was too much outcry and raising up in arms against the action, once it was known, then maybe the other States would get some breathing room and not be treated in quite the same manner.

He thought it would already be a done deal, before the other States even realized what was happening up here.

Lynn wondered how Juneau was fairing. Was the Capitol overrun and Anchorage, also? Would the current weasel in Office there even make a protest? Or would he just hand over the State?

After the evening meal, they listened to the small short wave radio set up in the living room. It took a while to find anyone on it. When they did, the news was worse than they expected.

Over the last few months, the military Bases in the State had seen a turnover in the personnel, leadership and soldier alike. Now they had been turned loose on Anchorage. Probably in Fairbanks, also, but the report they were hearing was from Anchorage. Packs of the soldiers were rampaging through the streets, downtown now looked like the news photos coming out of Beirut. Cargo planes were landing nonstop, dropping off more blue helmeted enforcers.

They were supposed to control the regular troops but ignored what was happening entirely. The National Guard Armories were being bombed. Some of the units had managed to escape, but were being hunted. None of the information was very good.

There was no report from the Interior of the State. They said subdued goodnights and Lynn went out to her bed in the garage.

During the night, the cats suddenly spooked away from her bed and roused her to some sounds inside the garage. Before she could reach a weapon, a solid body slammed into hers on the bed. A fist slammed into her jaw and she was out.

Lynn regained consciousness slowly and tried to identify the sounds she could hear and why her jaw ached so badly. It came back to her slowly and she tried to sit up.

Halya rushed to help her. "I am so sorry we didn't realize he got lose. He will never hurt you again though. I have water heating so you can take a shower. Come, put this robe on and let's go over to the house."

"What did he do?" then she gasped as she started to sit up and she knew what he had done.

Her legs felt wobbly as they made their way over to the house. Halya set the shower up and showed her how it worked, then left her to use it.

The water was hot and she used lots of soap, feeling like she would never be clean again. She knew that was just her mind, and that she would be fine, but at the moment, she wanted to go stick a knife in the man, or remove parts slowly.

When Lynn finally came out of the small bathroom, she did feel better. Halya led her over to the couch and wrapped a soft blanket around her. "I know it isn't cold, but maybe it will feel good, anyway. We should talk about what happened, then never speak of it again, unless you want to.

Lynn wasn't sure she wanted to talk about whatever had happened, but after thinking about it a few moments, she decided that yes, it probably would be better to know just what happened. "I really don't know what happened. The cats woke me up, I heard a sound and reached for the gun and something fell on me. I think I got hit."

She touched her jaw and realized it was swollen quite a bit.

"We thought he was tied well enough to be okay for the night. Gabe checked him for weapons and didn't find anything, but somehow he cut his wrists free, then got his ankles. I think he expected to be able to take you out first, then with your weapons, he could manage both of us." Halya said.

"Gabe went to check him one last time before bed and found him gone, then heard a sound from the garage and rushed over there with me right behind him. He was just getting ready to slash your throat when I got him with my knife." She showed Lynn her knife she kept in a sheath along her leg. "Gabe grabbed him in time to keep him from falling on you and dragged him outside. He was still alive, so I made sure he knew he was not going to be equipped to handle all those virgins promised him." here, she stopped and blushed a little bit. "Well, I suppose I could have done without doing that, but it seemed fitting."

"Thanks, I am glad you did that. I have been wishing I could have done that, myself. I think I will go over and make sure my cats are okay and cuddle with them a bit. Thank you for all you have done for me, and I do mean everything."

"Are you sure you want to go back out there tonight? It is okay if you want to stay in the house here. The couch is fine for sleeping." Halya offered.

"No, I will be okay. I need to go right back or I may never want to. Goodnight."

Chapter 3

Lynn walked slowly back over to the garage. Gabe met her at the door and asked if she was going to be okay. "Yes, I will be, this is just a bump in the road. It may slow me down for a time, but I will get over it."

After shutting and barring the door, she sat on the edge of her bed a few minutes. Pretty soon the two cats came out of hiding and came over to her. "Thanks, guys. You did wake me up, I was just too slow getting a gun out. I'll have to keep it handier after this."

She slid the revolver under her pillow and settled in to try sleeping through what was left of the night. She surprised herself by falling right to sleep and not even having any bad dreams about it. Maybe it was the thought of what Halya had done evened it out a bit.

She was up and dressed when a small tapping sounded on the garage door and she hurried over to open it. Halya stood there, looking uncertain. "How are you feeling this morning? I was worried maybe you were hurt worse than we realized as he did knock you out and we should have watched to make sure you didn't have a concussion or something."

"No, I feel fine this morning and need to start looking for somewhere to build myself some sort of shelter for the winter. Do you mind if I stay fairly close down here? Maybe we can help each other out once in a while."

"That was another thing Gabe and I talked about. We would like it if you stayed as close as you are comfortable with. The way it is looking, we may be the only people around here, for a while and any others that show up may not be ones we want to have around. So, yes, we would like to see you stay close. Breakfast is ready, if you would care to join us."

After breakfast, they walked up the valley a small distance to a pretty small meadow, with a rock bluff on one side and very large spruce and birch trees on the other side. The small river ran closer to the tree side than the bluff. Gabe said he could bring the backhoe up here after they checked to see if there were any of the invaders in the area to hear the motor. He thought near the rock bluff would be a great area to dig back into the bank and build a home similar to theirs in there. Lynn liked the area very much and it was close enough to Gabe and Halya that they could help each other out if needed.

Lynn walked back up the hill toward her home. She didn't leave the woods, just observed from a distance and it did not appear to have anyone in it. She did not want to take a chance on going in and salvaging anything as she didn't know if there would be booby-traps or surveillance of any sort. She backed away and checked out her newer pickup from a distance, also. It did not look like it had been bothered until she got to the other side and saw the door partly open. She did not go investigate any closer but walked back down to the old plow truck.

It started up immediately and she slowly edged it down through the trees, closer to her future home site. As long as she didn't rev it up, it was a very quiet vehicle. She got it close enough to see the rock bluff through the trees and stopped it under a canopy of spruce. Then she covered it again in the brown tarp. The akio had pulled along behind it fairly well, so now she had almost all of her supplies down here. It was going to be a very hard job, starting over and making do when she could not go buy something when needed. If her place remained unoccupied, she might go try to salvage some things from the sheds.

She used the grubhoe and started removing sections of moss and vegetation from the area she planned on building into. She knew her house wouldn't be as elaborate as theirs, but she could use ideas from the way they constructed storage into the walls.

She had most of the surface removed before Gabe made it up there with the backhoe. She was amazed to see how he camouflaged it. The yellow paint was not visible at all and assorted branches stuck out here and there, to break up the outline. He set up and immediately started work. After he was done on the excavation for her house, he dug a smaller hole over on the hillside downstream from the house to use for an outhouse when she got around to building one. Then he dug a trench between the two workings.

"It's a help, not having to carry out used water from the kitchen in the winter", he explained. He had a lot of sewer line and would bring some over to put in and they could cover that.

"I thought sooner would be best for using the equipment," he explained, "I think they are still on the way out, picking up everyone they find and won't start moving into an area until they are satisfied they have everyone rounded up or dead."

"That sounds reasonable to me. There has been someone around my other pickup, but I didn't go up to the house itself or touch the pickup. The old one is now parked right over there in the trees." She pointed.

"Wow, I would never have figured it would make it all the way down here. There are some pretty big gullies on this hill."

"Yes, but knowing where they are, I managed to go around the heads of them. I only hit a few trees," she laughed. "I think the trail will be pretty hard to find in a couple more days. Anything else I manage to get will have to be brought down on my back or the akio. I'm still thinking maybe I should try for the ATV."

"Where are the keys for it?"

"On the pickup keys, in my pack."

"Let me park the backhoe at the house and tell Halya what we are up to and let's go back up and check it out. It could be very handy to have down here in the future."

Lynn worked on evening up her future floor with the grubhoe and Gabe was soon back. He handed her one of the rifles they had picked up from the invaders, yesterday. "It's lightweight and the magazine is full, so see how you like carrying it. You should have it with you at all times."

"I do have my handgun on me all the time and a couple of knives."

"This is more intimidating and better range. Too bad we can't check them out for accuracy."

She looked it over and set the firing to single shot. "I don't like the spray and pray method of shooting. I like to make each shot count." she explained.

"I agree and a single shot is harder to pinpoint location, also."

When they reached the ATV, Lynn looked it all over from a distance, then a closer inspection. It looked exactly the way she covered it when she parked it out in the trees, before she left the house for the last time. It started right up and she pulled over near the house. She went around back and soon reappeared on the porch, unhooking the small solar panel array, then carrying everything over to the open window she had gained access through. Gabe carried everything over to the ATV as she unhooked the inverter and got the lights and battery.

Then it was on to the newer pickup. She didn't bother the doors, leaving them the way she found it. Not much was moved around in the back, so she took her Dutch oven and cooking supplies. There were several bags of dry food items and she loaded up the ATV. Some of her favorite books made it into the load, and she looked forward to having them with her. Gabe saw she had already removed the battery and included it on her 1st trip.

As she neared the greenhouse, she stopped and ran inside. She had the container of seeds and some of the garden tools with her. Then she headed back and grabbed the little Mantis. It wasn't much as a tiller but better than none at all, as long as the gas held out. She turned on the line from the rainwater tank to the soaker hose to water the growing stuff in the greenhouse, then started down the hill again.

This was a bonus trip and she was thankful to get as much more of her stuff as she could. While she had been in the greenhouse, Gabe loaded the pile of greenhouse panels stacked beside it, ready to expand the size of the present one. These were all things that might make the difference in just barely surviving or actually making a go of it in the future.

She could only hope no one moved into her home. Maybe she could get more of her food supplies that were left behind, thinking the jars would freeze and break if she had to spend the winter in minimal shelter. But if she managed an underground shelter, the jars should be fine.

As they unloaded their salvage, she asked Gabe what he thought of trying one more trip for canned food. He was ambivalent about it, knowing they would need the food and worried they were taking too many chances.

The idea of all that food tipped the balance and they proceeded back up the hill. They came around from a different direction this time and made it to the house without observing anything out of the way or different. They did still use the window as access. They used blankets and layered the jars in the akio with the blankets and clothes over and between for cushioning. Pretty soon they had a huge load and the boxes found were all full and tied onto the luggage racks of the ATV. They eased away from the house, slowly proceeding down the hill in yet another route around through the trees.

This trip was made super slowly. They hated the idea of breaking even a single jar. The extra blankets and clothes would be handy to have, too, so they tried to talk themselves out of another trip up, but finally went back up. They knew they were being foolish. This time it was the pile of lumber stacked behind the cabin that they targeted first. Then they filled all available space with more food.

Early the next morning, they heard traffic out on the road again. It all seemed to be coming from the north, headed for town. Just how many trucks and troops had gone north? They didn't hear anything stopping or restarting, so maybe they were safe for the time being.

They stayed quiet all day just in case. Not starting anything with a motor to let it be known they were in the area. Lynn worked with a bow saw, cutting down some fairly small spruce to use as studs in her home to be. The sound didn't carry as it would if using an ax and definitely not like a chainsaw. It took longer, but she had time.

She cut everything to 8 foot lengths and piled them near the construction site. Then she started cutting a bit larger trees and cutting 16 foot poles. These were stacked in a separate pile. She hoped they could figure out how to nail these and not have the sound travel too far. When Gabe and Halya walked over in the afternoon, they showed her how they notched and lashed the pieces together. It was actually stronger and would give in an earthquake better than a nailed wall. It seemed to have a lot in common with a yurt, only made of poles and buried.

This was going to be a small cabin. If she decided later to expand, she could. But for now it was more important to get under a roof and her supplies in a safe place.

Since her greenhouse was quite a ways from her house, she took a chance and went back up to check it and harvest what was ready.

She already had the zucchini harvested and stashed out in the woods and was picking cucumbers, being careful to leave some mature fruits of each item she harvested. It was hard to leave them behind, but she didn't want it to look like anyone was using it. She was even letting a few weeds grow in it. As she started out the back door with her bag of cucumbers and tomatoes, she heard voices coming down the hill from the house.

She quietly latched the door and slid down onto the ground, then scooted along through the brush she had not got around to cutting this spring.

Whomever was talking wasn't even trying to be quiet, but why should they? They were the superior force and everyone out here was already gone or dead. What did they have to fear?

They walked on by the greenhouse toward her newer pickup. She heard them laughing as they walked around it, checking the partly open door. Evidently it was booby-trapped and if anyone opened either door, the pickup would blow up. She wondered how good her insurance would be on that? She was glad she already had the battery out of it before the trap was set.

She stayed crouched down in the thick brush and her nose started itching. A mosquito found her and invited all its friends. Then her thigh started cramping.

By the time the two chatty cathies had moved back up the hill, she didn't know if she COULD move without howling. First she brushed off most of the mosquitos and rubbed her nose. The cramp was subsiding on its own, she thought, until she tried duck walking farther into the brush. She finally made it to some trees and inched around behind them, slowly easing herself upright.

She moved slowly and picked up all her harvest. Her pack was very heavy as she started wending her way around the hill to come in to her new home site from upriver. She knew fast movement would draw attention her direction and the chance of breaking sticks would increase the possibility of someone looking her way.

By the time she reached Gabe and Halya's home, her pack felt like it weighed more than she did. She wanted to contribute fresh vegetables to their menu. Halya was happy to see them, Gabe worried she had taken an unnecessary chance and maybe allowed someone to know they were in the area. She told him about overhearing the men talking about the pickup.

Chapter 4

While they ate dinner, they planned the jobs needing done to make her house livable as soon as possible. They would tack some of the membrane roofing around the outside walls, then start piling moss against it, then shoveling dirt. The roof poles would be lashed over the top as they worked on the walls. One of the greenhouse panels would do as a window in the front wall near the door. They would place a shutter over the outside that she could fasten to make it less easy to see.

The panel was eight feet long, so they decided to cut it in half and use half on each side of the front door. One side could be the kitchen side, the other, the living room area. It was all going to be one room, but she could use furniture to make individual spaces. Her bed would go across the back and hide the access to a small cellar behind the house.

They would use a couple of pieces of white plastic sewer line to place light tubes in her ceiling. Her stove pipe would go out beside a pile of stones on the bluff. There were some stunted spruce trees growing over the bluff that she hoped would dissipate the smoke. Nothing would hide the odor, but if the smoke itself wasn't a beacon, maybe the house would stay undetected.

Since it was still light all night, they worked outdoors at night and slept during the day. They hoped the occupying forces only patrolled during the day. The sounds of traffic seemed to bear this out. In the morning, they heard traffic headed north, in late afternoon, traffic all was headed south. Just what were they doing to have to keep traveling the road every day?

She raided her greenhouse again. Her watering system was still working with the soaker hoses from the rainwater tank. The tomatoes were ripening fast and she wanted to dry some. She took the weed burner from under the benches in the greenhouse. It had an igniter built in and she might need it someday. Her load was so heavy and difficult she almost just went straight home. Then thought better of it and still made a roundabout trek.

Her first symptom was the feeling dizzy and slightly nauseous while she worked. She didn't want to think it was even possible, so she ignored it and continued making her cabin winter worthy. She still used the bow saw to cut down some birch to have for firewood this winter. She dragged sections of the trees home, she could cut them up later, now she just wanted as big a pile as she could possibly get.

One area of the bluff made a natural partly enclosed cave so she leaned old dead poles she knocked down in the woods up against the bluff to keep it free of snow later on. As she cut the wood to length she stacked it in her makeshift woodshed.

After dragging a large log in, she felt so dizzy she was leaning against a tree, fighting the blackness when Halya found her. "What is wrong? Did you hurt yourself?"

She helped Lynn over to a stump and she collapsed onto it. "I didn't hurt myself, I just feel ill, like I have the flu or ate something bad. If I rest a bit, it goes away."

"Have you been overdoing it? Lifting things by yourself that are too heavy?"

"Not really. I'm used to working, Halya. I should be able to continue working. I just feel blah."

"Come to the house, I have some peppermint tea. Maybe that will help your tummy."

"That sounds good. I'll accept. I should try to dig up some of my plants and bring them down so we can have it whenever we want."

"You have peppermint plants? Yes, if we can get some started down here that would be great."

By the time they reached the house, Lynn felt fine but they still had some tea and visited a bit. Gabe and Halya were hand cutting firewood also and it was much more time consuming than usual. An ax would be heard as much as a chainsaw, so they were limited to the bow saws. They all knew they would be limiting how warm the homes were kept and probably still need to go cut any time the weather wasn't too cold. Cutting and hauling would help keep them warm.

Lynn and her cats were living in her cabin now and the cats were making sure no rodents joined them. All the roof poles were in place, the membrane fastened over it and overlapping the walls a bit and some dirt shoveled on, then some tarp she had brought, then more dirt and the vegetation she had carefully removed before the space was dug out with the backhoe. Now her home looked like it grew there. She piled rocks loosely around the front, so the wall didn't show so well. The door was set in a Z shaped angle in the wall, so it was harder to see. The rippled greenhouse panel windows gave a wavy view of the outdoors, from inside, but did not reflect light like glass can do on the outside. It wouldn't frost up as easily as a single pane of glass, either.

She planted trailing plants along the edges of the roof over the windows, to blend them in and more stones were placed around under them to make it appear more as small indents under the bank by the bluff. Now her floor needed something done to it. It was fairly level dirt, but that could change to a sea of mud in the right weather conditions. She placed poles across it and then split planks from a spruce tree for boards across the poles.

The large pole in the center of the room that supported the roof made a handy place to start a wall of shelves across for books and folded clothing as she reached her bedroom area. This gave a semblance of privacy and she prepared an area to use as a bathroom. She could stand in the large galvanized tub and use a bucket hanging from the ceiling as a shower. She made a bench seat to hold another 5 gallon bucket to use as a honey bucket for nights and winter. Once she hooked up a sink and drain in the kitchen, she could bail water from the tub into the drain. She made a support bench for an inverted traffic cone with a cover over it. It emptied directly into the pipe going to the outhouse to dump wash water.. New meaning for a cone head.

Next were shelves on the side she considered the kitchen. After she built them and placed her pots, pans and dishes on them, she felt like this could be a nice little home. It certainly had character.

She filled all the buckets with water that were now empty of the dry goods brought down. These she stacked by the back wall. Soon, she would be melting snow for water but she preferred to have as much water on hand as possible.

One evening after hearing the traffic head back to town and it was quiet for a while, she went back up to check her potato patch. The plants were dying down and the weeds were doing very well. After placing some weeds leaning out across the trail to the house and road she continued. She carefully dug and carried the potatoes over into the woods a bit, as she filled each bucket. It was not a large patch, so she finished before dark. The days were getting shorter now and soon it would be full dark at night, but she didn't want to use any light.

She packed the buckets in relays down the hill. It took most of the night. She harvested heads of cabbage by pulling every other head and smoothing the dirt back over the holes in the ground. The same with the onions and carrots. She might not make it home with everything tonight, but she would have it most of the way down the hill. She finally dug the mint plants.

She harvested the over ripe zucchini, tomatoes and cucumbers from the greenhouse to dry seeds from for next year. Then she picked the seed pods from the broccoli, turnips and radishes. These she could pick by touch as they all felt pretty much alike, no weeds felt similar and when it was time to plant, it would be interesting.

The sun was coming up over the hill as she finally carried the last load home. She plonked down on the bed and was out before she had time to think about it or change out of her clothes.

She awoke some time later with the cats sleeping against her, keeping her back warm. She felt disoriented a couple of minutes and the nausea returned. Her leg cramped and she took a drink from the bottle of water she kept by her bed. Grabbing a blanket from the shelf by the bed, she pulled it over her and they all resumed sleeping.

The next time she woke up, Halya was tapping at her door. When she let her in, Halya's eyes widened as she saw all the vegetables in the small room. "Wow, you should have said something, we could have helped."

"I thought it would be safer if only one of us was involved in case we got caught. There should be someone down here all the time, shouldn't there?"

"I don't know, but you did so much work. No wonder you are still sleeping. It is almost time for dinner."

"What? I'm sorry, I was supposed to come help work on the dryer racks today, wasn't I?"

Lynn explained why she brought the seed heads and the over ripe vegetables, then showed her how much other stuff there was to add to the food supply.

"If we are careful, we should have some to replant next season and keep stocked up on food."

"The cabbages can be eaten, but save the hearts, not cutting too deep and place the bottom in a glass of water. They will sprout and grow. They need the second year to make seeds. We need to dig some buckets of dirt to have for planting next spring. We will need to start a lot of the plants in the house to assure a crop."

They walked back over to Gabe and Halya's house and discussed trying to garden next season if things remained as they were, now. How they could plant in sheltered areas that wouldn't be noticed as cultivated plots and escape detection. It mostly depended on whether the occupying forces would be using drones and airplanes to check.

They turned on the radio to see if there was any news at all. They were surprised to hear someone broadcasting loud and clear. The message was not to submit, that there were resistance groups fighting. The broadcast ended by signing off as the "Alaskan Patriot." That cheered them up, but they didn't know whether to believe it or not. There was no reliable information given, but of course there couldn't be. It would just compromise location. The broadcast did say they would be at a different location each day of broadcasting.

If nothing else, it gave them hope. No one wanted to admit it, but each was feeling as though they might be the only free people left in the State. Now they knew there was resistance and evidently quite a bit of it in some areas.

There had not been any traffic on the highway for almost a week, so they decided to go see if they could salvage any more from Lynn's house and property. Part way up the hill, they separated and each came in to the house from a different direction. Nothing looked disturbed. Even the weeds were still where she placed them across trails and into the road. They were dried, but right where she placed them.

The house looked okay, but they did not go in the front door. Lynn led the way to the window she had used before while taking her solar panels. They helped each other in and left the window open for quick quiet egress if needed. They checked through the window to the front porch and the outside door was booby-trapped. They left it.

They systematically went through the house, gathering everything they could carry or stash in the woods to come back for later without coming to the house. As Halya and Lynn continued gathering things, Gabe started carrying it all farther down the hill. Lynn finally stood up straight and rubbed her back.

"Wow, the house is looking really nice and not cluttered like it usually is. Nothing like finally cleaning it up, just to not get to use it again."

"Maybe everything will be okay and you can move back home soon."

"I'm not going to hold my breath on that one, Halya, but the thought is good, thanks."

Chapter 5

After they returned to the valley, everything was piled in the middle of Lynn's new cabin.

"Dang, now this place looks as bad as the other one used to. I just like too much stuff. Thanks for helping me get so many of my books."

"I'll come back tomorrow and help you sort it all out and maybe we can find room for it all." Halya offered.

"Thanks. That would be great."

After they left, Lynn started putting the books on her shelves. At least that much could be done easily and fast. It also improved the look of the pile in the middle of the room. The extra blankets and sheets would be really nice to have on hand and who knew when or if she could ever buy any more.

She was still asleep when Halya returned the next day.

"I'm sorry, I should have been up. I've just been so darn sleepy lately. Every time I hold still, I doze off."

"We have all been working hard, trying to get everything ready for winter. Maybe once you relax, you can get rested up and not be so tired."

"I sure hope so, or else my body is intending on hibernating all winter like a bear. They have the right idea, just sleep it away. Maybe everything will be worked out by next summer."

"Maybe you have a bit of depression. That can cause sleepiness, too."

"Gee, why would anyone be depressed? Our own government is probably in cahoots with the invaders here, killing and imprisoning people. Everything is just fine, why would I be depressed? Oh, I am so sorry, you were just trying to be nice and I go ranting. Sorry." she wiped a tear from her face.

"Lynn, do you think you might be pregnant?"

"What? No, oh no, I can't be! No, that SOB can't have managed that, could he?"

"I'm so sorry, but yes, it is possible."

"All the signs seem to agree. The feeling ill, the tiredness, the sleeping all the time and the obvious one. I just thought maybe I was missing that because of being upset and working harder. Can we dig him up and cut him into littler pieces?"

"Lynn, I am so sorry we didn't get to him in time. I just don't know what to say."

"I will just consider it an accident and live with it. I certainly won't blame the child for what that person did. I refuse to call him the father. I'm not happy it is happening now, we don't need the added problems, but I will manage."

"I think I might be, also."

"Oh, wow, they will grow up together, then. That will be great for them. Are you happy about it?"

"Yes, we have been wanting a child. I just was afraid you would not be happy about yours and might not like seeing us enjoying ours."

"No, I don't like the circumstances of mine, but it is not the baby's fault and I can't say my timing is good to have one, with not even having a husband and our current outside problems. But we will be having two babies here and we will do the best we can for them. This way, yours will have an instant friend."

"I'm planning on telling Gabe tonight."

If the goofy grin she saw on Gabe's face the next day was any indication, he was extremely happy with the news. When he saw her, he tried not to look so happy.

"It is okay, Gabe. I am happy for you both. I would rather I wasn't along for the population explosion, but what's done is done and it isn't the baby's fault. At least I have an explanation for the way I have been feeling. It's almost a relief."

They buried a small pipe between the two houses with a wire through the center. The ends of the wires were fastened to a bell in each house. Lynn's was actually a small loud wind chime. It would stay chiming longer if rung. Primitive but it worked.

Now Lynn felt better that help was only a ring away. She had the chime set over by her bed, easy to reach.

The nights were getting darker and now there was frost some mornings. Lynn started carefully going back up, only as far as the greenhouse and slowly dismantling everything, bringing it all back down the hill. No one seemed to have ever paid any attention to it and nothing was ever harvested out of it, so she felt fairly sure she could take as much of the supplies as possible out of it.

She kept the weed burner over behind the bed. She wasn't sure why, but it was out of the way and yet she could reach it if she wanted to for any reason. It gave her a feeling of security.

Once there was any snow, she would not even attempt to come up the hill. Now she had all her gardening tools, the watering system and some of the growing beds with drains. She left it looking like she used the floor as her growing bed. She even took the thermometers.

She emptied the rest of the sheds she had until nothing useful to anyone else was left outside the house. She only wished she could manage even one more trip inside the house, but now it would show too well if anything else were missing. As it was, the house looked like a very neat person used to live in it. It was all nice and tidy with everything put away, nothing laying around. Certainly not like it looked when she lived there.

She grabbed more of the seed heads from vegetables in the overgrown garden. No telling what any of it was, but she would plant it and find out. It would all be a surprise.

The radio became an important part of each evening after they ate dinner. They would search until they found the evening broadcast, then listen. The reports told of finally contacting some HAMs in the Lower 48 and telling them what was actually happening up here. The newscasts down there only told of military exercises being held in Alaska, just like they were every year only on a larger scale so all tourism had been canceled. There was mention of people having rioted in Anchorage and it being held under martial law at present. No mention was made of the mass roundup of citizens all over the State.

There was definitely no mention made of the mass killing and relocations going on. The broadcaster said he didn't know whether anyone down there believed him or not, but he told them exactly everything he knew and told them to find out for themselves, it could happen to them next.

Then a voice cut in from Juneau. He told similar stories of what was happening there. With a spread out but easily located population, there had been bombings in the towns and mass killing. The old and very young were being killed immediately. The rest were being herded together to relocate. Suddenly there was the sound of gunfire and that voice was still. Several other voices were heard, then dead air.

Lynn, Halya and Gabe were very subdued after hearing that. They discussed it a bit but what as there to say? There was nothing they could do to help. Right now, staying alive and free was all they could do and hope to find some others to become a small community of free people. With winter coming on, they hoped the occupying troops would pull back.

The ground was white with snow the next morning and now they would have to be careful about making trails and leaving easy to find tracks. There had not been any searching done for the troop vehicle they had burned early on. They were not sure why, but were glad of it. The temperatures continued to drop, more snow piled up.

The next time they heard a radio broadcast, it was "Alaska Patriot" again and he told of a convoy of the military vehicles that somehow managed to get the fuel contaminated. The troops were stranded without cold weather gear or food supplies. They were attempting to march back to Fairbanks. Weapons were being dropped along the way as troopers froze hands trying to carry them.

Lynn was certain her attitude needed to improve, but she was glad they were having trouble. She hoped they all dropped along the way. Halya agreed with her.

Halya and Lynn made covers for their winter parkas out of white sheets. The covers had hoods and covered most of their parkas and legs. The sleeves were long and came down over their mitts if they wanted total white out. It would help them blend in, especially since Halya's parka was bright red.

Gabe was wondering how the people that were incarcerated were managing. Were they being cared for or were they suffering from the weather, also? Then both women felt the local people would certainly know how to manage better than these troops did, even if they were behind fences. Surely the local FEMA camps were built to Arctic standards?

There was the sound of distant gunfire to the north one afternoon. Then it tapered off, with an occasional shot now and then. Then silence.

When they left their yard, they followed moose trails as much as possible and tried not to wander off one until they were under the trees. Unfortunately, the moose didn't always go where they wanted to be. They stayed away from Lynn's home.

One moose trail went near the store so they followed it along and checked out the area around it. There was no sign of anyone living anywhere in the area and the road was not plowed nor were there any tracks from troops moving through on foot.

It looked like another snow storm was moving in, but slowly, so they decided to go check out the direction all the shooting was heard, earlier. They packed enough supplies that if necessary, they could stay out overnight, but didn't plan on it.

They walked single file, each stepping in the track in front. They would return the same way. They hoped the snow started on their way home, so they would leave very indistinct trails.

They were almost at the outer limit of how far they wanted to travel away from home when Gabe thought he saw something down on the road. They circled out around and came down into the road from the other direction. There had been a little bit of snow since they heard the shooting a day ago, but the signs were still there, to see what happened. One of the invaders' vehicles ran into another one of their own vehicles, evidently driven by two different factions.

There were bodies lying around on the roadway, but it looked like at least one went down over the bank, maybe dragging someone else. They stayed alert to anyone while they searched the vehicles and took out all the items they could use. Weapons were everywhere and the ammunition was in boxes in the vehicles, so they loaded down all the backpacks. Even if they had to cache some to make it home, they didn't want to leave it laying around here. The ammo was more important than having more weapons for themselves. The first aid kits were a bonus. However, if they found more local people, they would like to arm them better, too.

Only two of the bodies were dressed in winter gear. No winter gear was found in the vehicles either. Whether it had already been scavenged by someone but all the arms left, or they just didn't have any, was anybody's' guess. But since the weapons were all still there, probably they didn't have any. There was only snack food, no supply for overnight.

There were some duffle bags with fairly lightweight sleeping bags in them. Not enough for the amount of bodies lying around, so they started looking the bodies over better.

Two did not have uniforms on. They counted up and there were supplies for the others. So three, maybe four, people possibly took an invaders vehicle, the rest ran them down and rammed the vehicle, or they did.

They had all they wanted to salvage from the area so followed the tracks going over the side of the road. They watched both sides and checked behind themselves often. It was soon evident that there were two, one unconscious or badly injured.

Chapter 6

They walked quietly and stopped often, listening. Ahead and down lower, they thought they heard something in the brush. They waited.

The sounds slowed down, then went still, also. Great, now what were they supposed to do?

Gabe motioned for the women to hold still and wait, he would be right back. He dropped his pack, pulled his white cover completely over his sleeves and hood and slowly eased down the hill. Soon he was out of sight.

The women dropped their packs, and sat on them. The break was welcome. Lynn was almost dozing when she heard a whisper of sound right behind her and Halya. She threw herself over Halya and knocked them both over on the ground. The young man behind them sprawled flat and both women jumped on him, soon having him disarmed and slightly damaged but restrained.

"Aww, I wasn't going to hurt you, I just wanted to make sure who you were." he whispered.

They were not about to take chances, he was staying tied up.

When Gabe got back, he didn't see their prisoner at first. "Come on, there is an injured man down the hill farther that needs some help."

"What about this one?"

He jumped as the fellow sat up. "That's my Dad. He really needs someone to fix him up better. I tried, but I don't have any supplies with me." the young man said.

Gabe helped him up and looked at the women when he found the man was tied up like a present.

"We wanted to be sure which side he is on before we undid him to wander around." Halya said.

"I guess just saying which side I'm on probably isn't enough, huh?" the young man said while smiling at her.

"Nope. We can't take chances. But Gabe seems to believe you, so that is good enough for me. Lynn?" Halya said.

"I'll go along with whatever you two decide. I think if he was with the invaders, he would have some uniform or not as good of winter gear as he has." Lynn replied.

Since he was dressed pretty much the same as they were, he really didn't look as though he were with the other group. Local's outfits were a mishmash of old military surplus and assorted finds at the dump. The invaders all wore new looking uniforms and blue helmets. Their weapons were a lot fancier, also, although now, Gabe, Halya and Lynn all carried one of their rifles and had one of their handguns besides their usual ones. The young man also had one of the rifles and handguns besides an older model hunting rifle and a couple of handguns the women had taken when they first searched him.

When they reached the injured man, Lynn wondered how he had survived this far. His color was terrible, some of the corpses up the hill looked in better condition. Evidently no bones were broken, but he had been hit by bullets in a few places and looked like he suffered a beating also.

One good thing about the cold, it stopped bleeding and also some of the bruising from getting worse. They could ask questions later, now they needed to get home as the snow was starting to increase and evening was sneaking up on them. Then the wind picked up and started swirling the snow around them.

It would be good for hiding their trail, however just making it home could now become a problem. The injured man needed tending, but not in their present location. The young man had fashioned a travois of sorts to drag him this far and it seemed to have worked, so they continued on the same way. All they could hope was that the snow storm filled in all sign of their passing.

The young man introduced himself as Simon and said his Dad was James. He didn't mention last names but at least now they had names for the faces.

Simon and Gabe pulling together made much better time with Halya and Lynn as point and rear guard. All extra gear was piled on James on the travois so their hands were free to use their weapons if needed.

They were almost home when a young bull moose trotted across the trail in front of them. He didn't notice them but was paying attention to the trail behind him. They immediately stopped back under the trees where they didn't show and soon a pack of wolves trotted into view. They were in no hurry, they knew where the moose was and the longer they kept him moving, the easier their final assault would be. They ignored the people standing and crouched under the trees, they were single minded in the pursuit of dinner.

Lynn felt the baby move for the first time, while crouched under a tree watching a pack of wolves. She marveled how much it reminded her of butterfly wings fluttering.

Halya touched her arm to let her know they were ready to proceed. The two women smiled at each other, sharing a moment, then it was back to getting home through the thickening gloom.

They had circled around and came back up the valley to reach Halya and Gabe's home first. Halya hurried in to stoke up the fire and light some lamps. Gabe and Simon untied James from the travois and half carried him into the house. While they were doing that, Lynn went to her home and got her fire going good again, lit a light to have on when she came back and went back to see if she could help with the injured man.

She came in as they were removing his outer gear, and he was laying on a cot they put near the heater and a light. The wounds were not bleeding and they had not reopened any by moving him around. If there were exit wounds, he would probably be better off if they left the wounds as they were. None required stitching.

The beating was more of a worry. The bruising was intensive and his face was badly swollen. All they could hope for was no internal damages. They applied salve to the open wounds and lightly bandaged him up, then covered him with clean sheets and blankets after washing off as much of the blood as they could. He still remained unconscious and that worried all of them. Now all they could do was wait and keep him warm. If he seemed at all conscious, they could start spooning in some liquids. He would need to replace all he had lost. Too bad they didn't have IV solutions and supplies.

Then Gabe thought of the first aid supplies they had taken from the disabled transporters. He went out to check the load of supplies still around the travois. The first aid boxes were under everything else, of course, but there they were. He brought them in to thaw. Luckily, the directions in the box and manual were in English also, along with all the other languages represented.

Soon an IV was in place and Halya had a warm meal prepared. As they ate, Simon told them how he and his Dad happened to get in this predicament.

James got caught while hunting. His first wound was a minor flesh wound, but one of the captors seemed to enjoy beating someone that could not fight back as the others held him during the beating. Simon had seen most of it, before going for help. The other two locals had stashed one of the invaders' vehicles early on and they now decided to use it to follow and rescue James.

They caught up with the other vehicle near where both were, now, on the road and rammed into it, pushing it around in the road. They were ready and opened fire as soon as they got stopped. They thought they had it all under control when the other passenger in the front seat of the other truck stepped out and shot James and the other two locals. James had been unable to stand upright and was slowly toppling over when he was hit, so he just fell on over, not as badly wounded.

Simon was manning the gun on the vehicle and finished off the rest of the invaders. Then he panicked, not knowing whether there would be more invaders showing up soon or not, so started dragging his Dad away from the scene. Once out of sight, he fashioned the travois and loaded James onto it. The first night was terrible and he didn't dare build a fire.

Then he heard some sounds behind him and went back to see what it was. Oh, by the way, there were 2 quarters of moose under his Dad on the travois all this time, so they might want to bring them in before they froze.

He thought the warmth from the meat would help keep his Dad from freezing as he got him away from the area, he just couldn't manage more than the two quarters though. Gabe laughed and said he wondered just how much James weighed while dragging him here. He didn't look to be a fat person but the travois was really heavy.

The fresh meat would be welcome. Gabe and Simon went back out to retrieve the meat. "Sorry I didn't have time to skin it out." Simon apologized as they carried it in.

"Oh, we can manage that, I was wondering how we were going to get meat with those people around. I even considered following the wolf pack and taking part of their kill." Gabe told him.

"Maybe we should, anyway. Who knows when the chance for meat will come our way again?"

Lynn and Halya started work on the meat as Gabe and Simon prepared to go back out. Gabe asked if they could take Lynn's akio and she said yes.

Gabe got his crossbow from their bedroom and they started out to follow the wolves. If possible, no gun shots would give away their location. He packed some snares also.

When they returned many hours later, they had a lot of meat, a dead wolf and all the snares were in place out around the remains of the carcass. They placed the snares far enough back so birds and small scavengers should not be a problem.

They could check the scene from a distance with binoculars without leaving a trail themselves near the kill area. The moose had still been alive when they caught up with the pack, making a stand against a rock ledge but was too badly injured to leave alive to suffer. They killed the moose with the crossbow and just reloaded when the large wolf decided it was his kill and jumped it.

The crossbow took care of that, also and they hurriedly skinned off the back and upper legs of the moose, leaving the lower legs and gut pile intact in case it was seen from the air before the wolves or snow finished the job. After the akio was loaded, they set the snares out and about on possible ways to reach the carcass.

They would check tomorrow to see if they caught anything. Tonight, they were getting some sleep. The meat would be fine in the garage until tomorrow.

Chapter 7

The next morning, they were happy to see that James appeared to be improving. His color was much better and so far no sign of fever. Gabe started another IV drip and they kept the fire going so he wouldn't catch a chill.

They started cutting up the meat, some was started soaking in marinade to dry for jerky. Lynn brought over her manual steak cuber and made some cubed steaks, breaded them and fried with cream gravy for dinner.

The bones they were roasting to boil for soup stock made a wonderful aroma in the cabin. The potatoes, onions and carrots roasted in the pan with the bones made a great side dish for the steaks. After the vegetables were removed from the pan, water was added and the bones continued to cook. The broth was turning a rich brown, so when the voice from the cot asked for something to drink, they took over a cup of the broth with a glass of water.

Simon and Gabe helped James sit up and braced him with pillows before handing him the glass, then the cup. After quenching his thirst with the water, he sipped the broth. Once the broth was gone, he said he only woke up because he dreamed there were steaks and gravy.

Lynn prepared a plate for him and as she handed it to him, she was looking into a pair of bright blue eyes in the middle of the badly bruised face. Under all the battering and bruising, he was an attractive man.

Just who was this Angel of Mercy actually bringing him a steak? James looked at her as she approached. She was fairly tall, well rounded and a pleasant friendly face. Some would consider her mouth a bit too wide, but it suited her face and usually seemed to have a smile on it. Her eyes were hazel and changed with her moods. He felt as though he had known her forever, yet would never fully know her. He smiled to himself, he didn't even know her name. Maybe that fellow had hit him harder than he thought.

Halya brought over a bit more of the broth for him to sip on as he ate. He moved carefully as his injuries were very painful. His ribs felt like an elephant had stomped on him. He hated to think what he looked like, his face hurt from the inside, it must be painful to look at, but these two women didn't flinch away and tended to him. Each had her own beauty, to him they looked like angels.

His son came over to check on him and he was pleased to see that the young man was unhurt. He asked about their two companions and was saddened to hear they were both dead. The whole attack was over in a few minutes at most but at the time, felt like it was taking forever and moved in slow motion. He still felt bad that he was the reason the other two were dead. If he had not been caught without a hope of surviving resistance, he would have just fought on, rather than have them be killed saving him. But the first shot had knocked him out and when he regained consciousness, he was already restrained and then the beating had begun on the pretext of questioning him.

When he heard a motor rev behind them later, he braced himself and the collision didn't hurt him except the damage already done during his beating. He took great pleasure in taking care of the man responsible for it. He should have made sure the passenger was dead instead of just leaving him slumped over in his seat. That lapse in judgment cost two good lives and messed him up even more than he had been.

Gabe and Simon went back out to check the snares, late in the day and returned with two more wolves. They were propped near the door to thaw and skin later. They would have need of the furs.

Lynn was tired so said goodnight and went home to get some sleep. She was still sleeping more than she usually did, but most of the nausea had passed. The baby was moving more often now after she first noticed it and she found herself talking to it. She was starting to thicken around the middle, but being as active as she and Halya both were, they were not gaining much weight.

They were still falling trees every day and dragging the wood in for fires. She had everything in her makeshift shed cut to length and didn't want to use it until the weather turned bad or she got to the point of not being able to. She kept a large supply inside her cabin, but didn't use it, either, for the same reason. If she was ill or it was too cold, she didn't want to have to go out anyway or freeze.

With snow on the ground and a clear night, she could see well enough outside to carry in firewood without auxiliary light. Once she had the wood in, she lit a lamp and started preparations for bed.

The curtains were pulled across her windows so no light would show from outside. A small pot of rice was started then set back on the edge of the heater. It would slow cook and be her breakfast and some mixed with dry food she still had for the cats would be their breakfast, also. They added voles to their diet almost daily as the voles kept coming into the cabin.

Once she finally was in bed, she couldn't sleep. She felt so tired but just couldn't relax enough to doze off. She got up and was looking out the window when she saw a shadow move out in the trees. As she watched, more shadows moved and she quickly rang the bell to let Gabe and Halya know there was a problem. She just hoped they didn't just run over to see if she was okay. She should have known they would be cautious.

The shadows came on out into her yard, but apparently didn't see her home. She hurriedly dressed and pulled out her new weapon. She quietly opened the door and slipped out into the night, right behind the 4 men making their way down the valley. By the details she was able to make out, they were not locals. The helmets gave them away and they were talking to each other as they slowly walked. They were freezing and not dressed for their job.

As they passed by Gabe and Halya's, Halya stepped in beside her, following them. Gabe was over on one side, under some trees and Simon on the other, by the cabin. Halya and Gabe understood what they were saying, so listened in as they complained about the cold, the people and the job.

This was supposed to be a quick take over, during the middle of summer. Who knew these people would be so scattered out and unwilling to surrender? When the operation had been planned, the number of residents for the entire State was well under a million and only a few towns and small cities. That should have simplified everything. In Europe, everyone lives in the towns and may work out of town, but still, home is in a small community of some sort or at least very close by. These people here thought nothing of living by themselves hundreds of miles from anyone else. It was not natural nor normal. Then, when they were ordered to hand over their guns, they actually just started shooting.

The sheer size of the State boggled the mind. What was with the no roads? This was supposed to be part of America, didn't they all live like kings here and never get their hands dirty doing menial work? There certainly had been preconceived notions about the entire operation and occupation. A quick take over, set up the reeducation centers, dispatch anyone not settling in and behaving and relocating people from the Mideast into the towns and cities already here. It looked so good on paper.

As the 4 men complained and Halya translated to Lynn, Lynn almost laughed. Then one of the men smelled the wood smoke and shushed the others. As they went on the alert, Gabe shouted something to them in their own language. One of the men whirled and started to fire but Halya shot him first. Then the rest of the men started running. Lynn knew it was necessary to shoot them, but had a hard time actually shooting someone that was trying to get away. Then she thought of what would happen if anyone got out to the others and they came back.

She shot the man closest to Simon. Then couldn't get a clear shot at anyone else, so just followed along behind. Then there was a scream, ahead of them as one of the men ran into a set wolf snare. The scream choked off. Then another.

When they reached the snares, one man was caught by his leg and evidently his companion would rather just knife him than save or leave him alive, but then stepped into another snare and now turned on them as they came into view. Gabe shot him. Then they released the snares and picked them all up. They would leave the men where they lay and only took the weapons. Maybe the scavengers would take care of the rest.

As they walked back home, Halya asked Lynn how she happened to see the men. Lynn told her and she laughed a little to think insomnia had its good points. To think, they put her farther up the valley thinking to protect her, and she was the one to see the first invaders. Who would have thought they would come from that direction.

Gabe suggested they may have been remnants of the ones trying to get back to town on foot that they had heard about on the radio and maybe followed their trail from the ambush where Simon and James came over the bank. From some of the talk he overheard, it sounded like that, to him.

Lynn went on over to her home to try sleeping again. This had not been what she had in mind when she went to bed early. Now she was wide awake and a bit chilly, so she sat in front of the fire, relaxing and the next thing she knew, it was getting daylight and she had a major crick in her neck.

She ate her breakfast and fed the cats. They usually gave her a pained look, before eating it. This was not what they expected for breakfast but since it was there…and proceeded to devour it all.

When she got over to Gabe and Halya's, they were preparing to make the jerky. Since it was too cold to smoke outside, they would have to just dry it over the wood heater. So they were building racks to put the strips of meat on. She helped on that while Gabe went outside to get more wood. Simon went with him. They were gone a while, and when they came in, they explained they moved the bodies here on down to be near the other two. Then they found some dead trees and brought home dry wood. Part was unloaded by Lynn's house.

The meat looked ready to dry, so they started hanging it. They would move the racks over the stove after the meat stopped dripping. For now, they had rags on the floor under it to catch the drips. Outdoor smoking was so much easier. The other reason they didn't even want to try outdoor smoking was the odor. Smoking meat smells so good and the scent on the air really travels. Even just wood smoke is noticeable, the man last night only noticed the smell, not the actual buildings.

James looked much better this morning. His face was still swollen and discolored, but the skin not bruised didn't look grey anymore and he didn't look like one of the corpses. He wanted to get up and help, until he actually tried to get up, then he was willing to stay on the cot, although he did ask if the pillows could be put behind him so he was more upright. Simon and Gabe managed without hurting him too much although he lost a couple shades of healthy color.

Lynn brought over her manual meat grinder and they set it up to make some burger from the smaller pieces of trimmings from the moose. James asked if he could be helped over to a chair, he thought he could turn the grinder for them as they fed it.

Gabe and Simon were trying to get more wood in as it looked like bad weather would be hitting soon. So Simon helped his Dad to a chair at the table and he did manage to turn the handle for quite a while, then he fed the hopper while Lynn turned the handle. He hated to say it, but she was stronger than he was at the present. Then delicate looking little Halya came over and took her turn at it and also did a faster, better job on turning the handle. James told them he hated to think that two ladies could do better than he could.

Chapter 8

Gabe and Simon came in to get warmed up and Halya had some soup ready on the stove. Everyone stopped and had a bowl with some bread and got better acquainted while they ate. Lynn asked Simon and James if they knew Rich and Travis and they did. They said Rich recovered very well from his wound, earlier in the summer.

They used to live out beyond Travis's place a few miles, so just next door neighbors. Travis came over to let them know about what was happening in town. They would have been caught right away as they were planning a trip to town the day after he told them.

When Lynn went home to start her wood cutting for the day, she was surprised to find a large pile cut, ready to stack in her makeshift woodshed. She still went ahead and cut some more so she would be ahead even more. Then she stacked the wood inside and loaded even more in her house. It was starting to feel like a second woodshed. She appreciated it the nights nausea had her in its grip.

When she returned to Gabe and Halya's, Halya was cooking dinner, so she pitched in to help. The potatoes were still nice and firm, so they ate a lot of baked potatoes. Later, when they got shriveled, they would probably boil more with the skins on, for the nutrition in the skins, but they wouldn't look very appetizing. They just needed to save enough to sprout and grow this coming summer.

By the time Lynn walked back to her cabin for the evening, the snow was coming down hard and the temperature was dropping. By morning, her nose hairs froze as she stepped outside. She didn't want to check the thermometer and know how cold it was, she already knew it was cold. At least the wind stopped. She hurried and cut a couple of trees and dragged them home. She would cut them up later, she was cold. She walked over to Gabe and Halya's and got there in time to turn the jerky as it was drying very well on the racks.

James was able to get up and only winced a bit as he moved around. His face was getting more colorful as the bruises started fading into greens and yellows. A lot of the swelling had gone down so he was more comfortable now. He was already asking what he could do to help.

Gabe and Simon were cutting wood almost every day, even in the cold, until they broke a saw blade in a frozen tree. It was so cold the metal was becoming brittle. Then they went around and knocked over all the dead trees they found and dragged them in, too. Finally they decided just maybe they had enough for a while or this place was going to look like a log jam.

There was no noticeable aerial surveillance going on, at least if there was, it was super quiet. They hoped that meant there was none. However, as the cold held on, they thought maybe the invaders were not out and about. No sound of motors on the road could be heard. Gabe and Simon followed a moose trail up to the road and it was not plowed at all, nor were there any tracks of vehicles showing. They were just out of sight of the road when they heard the sound of a snow machine. They both crouched down and waited. The snow machine came around the corner from the north. The operator was dressed in a hodge podge of winter gear, just like they were, so Gabe motioned for Simon to stay back and he stood up and walked toward the road. The snow machine slowed and stopped back a ways. The driver raised his helmet and Gabe had seen him before, he just didn't know his name. Then another head popped up over his shoulder, there was a woman riding on the back.

"My wife is in labor and we were trying to find a ride to town." The man said.

"You really don't want to go there, they will lock you both up, if you do." Gabe replied.

"What for? We haven't done anything wrong."

"Have you been to town since early in the summer?"

"No, we live out beyond the Hoot, up on an old patented mining claim near the base of the Sawtooths. We went in, the first of summer and stocked up and haven't been back since, why?" the man replied.

"Well, I'm not sure how to tell you this, but we have been invaded as a rogue State and so-called peacekeepers have taken over. Killing all the elderly and very young, putting everyone else in camps for work and retraining. Did you see the wrecked vehicles up the road a ways?"

"Yes, I wondered about those."

"That was two of their rigs. They shot the folks down at the store and loaded up everyone else they could find, out here. It's been a mess."

The man slumped a bit on the machine and his wife made a sound, behind him. He looked a little wild eyed by the time he looked back up.

"Just what are we going to do? She isn't wanting to just go home. We thought we could do this on our own, at home, but the first pain hit and she was gearing up to get out of there. We brought stuff for it, after it gets here, but it is the getting here that has us in an uproar."

"You can come on down to the house and we can see about helping out, if you like, but it isn't safe going to town."

"We? There are other folks here?"

"Yes, my wife and another lady, plus two other men are living down the hill. You two are welcome to come on down, if you want and we can give you a hand."

There was some conversation on the snow machine and then another yip of pain. The man turned back to Gabe.

"I guess there isn't a lot of choice, she thinks it is almost here and we sure don't want to have it on the road. Let's get down to your place."

Gabe and Simon started down the hill as fast as they could go on the cross country skis they were wearing and the snow machine was right behind them, idling along.

When they reached the house, Halya and Lynn stepped out with weapons. Then the woman let out another yip of pain and everyone jumped into action. Gabe told Halya they were about to have a birth so she motioned Lynn and they both went indoors to ready up the cot. James was seated on a chair in the kitchen and stayed out of the way.

They put plastic on the cot, then a sheet and towels over it. They stoked up the fire. Lynn started a pot of water boiling. Halya asked her why and she said that is what they always do in books and the movies. The men had the woman indoors by then and immediately all but her husband disappeared. Halya told him to help her get undressed and on the cot. The woman was obviously close to wanting to push and finish this job. After she was laying down, Halya placed a warm soft sheet over her upper body and asked if she wanted anything. The woman said an ax, she was going to fix Jesse here, and then she was going to die, she never wanted to see his ugly face again, this baby was killing her.

Halya suggested Jesse go back outside with the other men. He was more than willing to comply. He was muttering about she seemed happy about the baby up until a few hours ago.

Lynn gave the woman a sip of water then held her hand as another contraction hit. Halya found a dresser drawer and lined it with a soft blanket, then placed another next to the stove to be nice and warm for the baby and a soft towel to wrap it in, first.

James kept his mouth shut and out of the woman's line of sight. He figured any man would be fair game right about now.

The woman started pushing on the contractions now, but nothing was happening. No crowning. Nothing. James washed up his hands and stepped over, "Maybe I can help."

He had tied a handkerchief over his lower face as a mask, and he sat down on a block of firewood at the foot of the cot. The draped sheet hid him from the woman, but by now she really didn't care who was there, she just wanted this over with. After the next contraction, he felt inside with his fingers and found the baby had one arm twisted around. He quickly pushed it back and she immediately gave a giant push. The baby's head crowned and with another push, it was halfway out. James caught it as it slipped the rest of the way out. A little boy. He wiped its face off, then covered it with a soft towel and placed it on the mother's stomach. Then he sat back and waited for the placenta. Halya brought over some clean string she had dipped in that pot of boiling water, and James tied off the cord. Then he snipped it. Halya placed the wrapped baby up into the mother's arms.

The woman was so happy to have it over with that she laughed and asked James what his name was. He told her and she said she was naming the baby after him. He got flustered and stammered, "Thanks."

He washed up and made his escape back to the kitchen.

Lynn placed a pad under the woman after removing all the stained towels. They were put in a tub behind the stove with melting snow water in it, to soak and clean, later. Then after she was sure the woman was well covered and the warmed blankets were over her, she went to the door and told the men they could come back in now.

They had been over at the garage, moving things around and getting a good fire going in the stove. It was going to be too crowded for everyone to stay in

Gabe and Halya's house. They set up a couple more of the cots. James might be able to walk over, if they helped him. He and Simon would move over there for the time being.

When the men came in, they carried another folding cot. Simon had been sleeping on the floor, but they thought maybe Jesse would like to sleep next to his wife, if she no longer wanted to kill him. The baby would be placed in the drawer on a box, between them.

Once everyone was back inside, Jesse introduced his wife to them. She smiled shyly as he told them she was the love of his life, Marilee. She told him she wanted to name the baby after James, the man that was responsible for him being born. Jesse looked at her and a hard look at James, "What? How is he responsible? You never set eyes on him until today."

Halya explained about the baby needing help and James knew what to do. Jesse relaxed and grinned. "So, since you are on such good terms with my wife, you going to get up at night with the baby?"

"Nope, I did my part. Now it is back at you to take up the rest of the job. Besides, I'm sleeping in the garage, so doubt if I even hear him."

"I don't think we can stick the poor baby with both our names, another Jesse James is not needed in this world. So how are you planning on doing this, woman?" he turned to his wife.

"Oh, I didn't think of that. How about James Jesse, then he will have both of your names for the two men responsible for his life." She answered.

"James Jesse Pitman, that don't sound bad together. Okay, that's what it is." he kissed his wife on the cheek and she swatted him.

"That's what started this whole thing, so get out of here. Not happening again." she told him.

He sat down on the floor beside her and held her hand as they watched the sleeping face of their new son. Soon she dozed off with the baby and Halya carefully placed the baby in the waiting drawer. The warmed blankets around him cocooned him in warmth and he slept on.

Chapter 9

James was sitting on his kitchen chair again, worn out from just the small amount of activity. Jesse came over and held out his hand in thanks. After shaking hands, they sat in comfortable silence a while, just watching Marilee and the baby sleep. James told Jesse he should be asleep too, as tonight, the baby might not be so obliging.

"I'm just trying to remember if I turned off the lights when I left home this morning. I'm pretty sure I shut the door. I'm going to have a time, until I get back and know everything is okay. My brother and his wife live a bit farther beyond us, but Marilee wanted a real doctor. She refused to just go over to their place or have me get them to come over. If she was having trouble though, she was probably right to make me come this direction. None of us have any medical knowledge at all. I need to pick up a book at least."

"Glad to have been of help. The baby may or may not have eventually moved around of his own accord, but it was probably better that they didn't have the extra strain on either of them. I used to volunteer as an EMT before I moved up here."

"So what happened to you? You don't exactly look up to being up and around yourself."

"I got captured while I was out hunting. Pretty stupid, really. Here I was hunting a moose and got shot, myself. I didn't even know anyone else was around. I need to bone upon my hunting skills before I try that again. First they shot me, then beat me half to death, just because they could. They were not questioning me or anything I refused to cooperate on, I never got the chance, not that I would have anyway, so the officer in charge probably made a good call on that one."

"So there really is an invasion of "Peacekeepers" here in Alaska just randomly picking everyone up or killing them? That just don't seem possible and I almost didn't come on down after Gabe told me that, up on the road. If the road had been plowed at all this winter, I would not have even thought he was more than some kook trying to kidnap us or something. Although why anyone in their right mind would want to kidnap us is beyond me. I don't think there is much market for an obnoxious male, his equally obnoxious wife and a newborn in this brave new world."

"Your kind of people is just what is needed though, whether or not there is a market or not. Ones that are too nice won't last long around these animals. Gabe told me what they caught some of them doing down at the little store the day they came out here, the first time. He and Lynn made sure those would never do that again, but they are certainly not a change for the good."

Jesse didn't think he wanted to know what they had seen. "Are most of the 'Peacekeepers' from a certain area known for their zeal?"

"That's one way to put it, but yes, they are."

"Damn. I'm glad Gabe happened to be at the road and we happened to stop. I hate to think what would have happened if we had gone on to town. We would probably all be dead now if we were lucky or wishing we were, if not."

Halya and Lynn were preparing an evening meal while the two men talked. Halya told Jesse it was best not to even think of what would have happened to Marilee and the baby, it would only give him nightmares and the reality would have been even worse than he could imagine.

Lynn prepared some more tenderized steaks, but made a brown gravy from some of the broth made on the roasted bones. The fresh vegetables were about all gone from her garden and greenhouse, but they all enjoyed the few that were left.

After cleaning up from dinner, Lynn walked home again. James and Simon were going too, so they walked together as far as the garage. James leaned heavily on Simon by the time they reached the garage and Lynn opened the door for them. She told them goodnight and went on to her home. The fire was still going enough to just add more wood for the night. She used a candle to read by, for a while, but soon caught herself nodding off so blew it out and managed to sleep soundly.

She had some nausea that morning when she woke up, so held very still and tried to think of anything but her stomach and food. It didn't work, she barfed in the bucket kept handy be the bed.

Lynn was still looking a little green when she knocked on the door at Gabe and Halya's. Halya had the same expression, so they smiled at each other and got the day's work under way. The buckets of snow melt water on the heater were hot enough to do laundry and they set up two tubs away from the cot that Marilee still occupied. She sat up and told them she was not going to lay around while they cleaned up her mess. Then she found she wasn't quite up to scrubbing out towels on a scrub board just yet.

She sat down on the couch and looked disgruntled that she wasn't already back to her former self. Lynn told her anyone that just traveled as far as she had on a snowmobile while in labor was no wimp. Just relax a bit and enjoy the extra hands helping out while she could. Jesse was already talking about heading home. He was worried that the rest of his family that lived near him would get caught by accident, not knowing about the invaders. After he explained his reasoning, the others tended to agree with him, they needed to get home as soon as possible.

Lynn offered enough of her gas to fill up their snowmobile for the trip home. They had extra with them, but would need it and she didn't know how long it would stay good. She did have her small generator and the chainsaw and tiller, but never was feeling confident enough to use any of them. There was always the fear someone would hear them.

The following morning, they loaded up the baby and all the stuff Lynn and Halya gave them to help out on the way home and left. The snow was pretty deep, but if they stayed to high ground, they should be fine. Jesse was using a map for the trip home, trying not to make more tracks on the road. The snow was slacking off as they left and they were worried anyone flying over would find where they were going and where they had been. The new route would cut many miles from their trip if all went well.

By the middle of the afternoon, the wind was blowing and snow started up again. Everyone hoped Jesse and family were already home or making it just ahead of the storm moving in. They had told Jesse about Alaska Patriot on the radio, so he was going to try setting up the old radio he had in one of his storage sheds. He thought maybe his brother would be able to make it work.

Two nights later, they heard another message from Alaska Patriot on the radio. He said the intruders were pulling back to the Anchorage bowl area, hauling the inmates from the camps around Fairbanks in rail cars down to the huge camp west of Anchorage. There were still some of the Alaska National Guard roaming around hunting invaders down like vermin. The Alaska Militia were doing their best to thin them out, also.

He said anyone wanting to join could, but it was hard to find the groups as they traveled continuously and kept under cover as much as possible. He warned of possible aircraft spraying poisons or disease over the Interior of the State. They started to, in Southeastern, but the wind drifted some across the Border into Canada and caused an incident. So if they heard any planes flying over, get in a building and stay there. He didn't know how long it took to dissipate. Keep all exposed skin covered if possible, leave clothes worn outside, out of the house. These people were not averse to killing everything and everyone off.

James said he hoped Jesse was home and had the radio working. The rest agreed. Lynn hoped someone in the Lower 48 would hear about all this and raise a stink. Make people down there wake up to what government was doing. They would be next if it worked okay here. They were a very subdued group that broke up for the evening. No one wanted to think about what could be coming next.

The days settled into routine with the two added to their small group. The couple of days with Jesse and Marilee had added excitement to their winter. Lynn thought she could do without the added excitement. She had quite enough to think about already.

She was going through all her clothes, putting older T shirts over on the side to cut into diapers and assorted baby needs. The sleeves would work as personal clothes for herself. She wasn't too sure just what a baby would need. But figured she would make sleepers of a sort and diapers, plenty of diapers. Without disposables and plastic pants to put over the cloth ones, there was going to be a need for all the other little clothes and blankets that she could manage and she would probably be doing laundry ever couple of days even then.

Some of her softer blankets were getting repurposed as baby blankets. She wasn't cutting them down too much as she would have nothing to replace them with as the child grew. She was hoping everything had been resolved in the near future, but wasn't going to waste supplies on wishful thinking. Knowing how fast government worked in the best of times, now that the unthinkable had happened and government was their main enemy, they could not depend on anything working right in the future.

She asked Halya what she was doing to prepare and Halya got an odd look and whispered, "Oh no, I haven't even started."

"I've been making diapers out of old T shirts and sweatshirts. I have a lot, so if you need to, we can share." Lynn offered.

They decided to walk over and see just exactly how many were made and how many they would need. Halya looked over the shelves now stocked with baby supplies and laughed. "Wow, you must be thinking you don't want to wash clothes very often."

Lynn showed her that a lot were made in different sizes and she thought maybe she had enough to not worry too much for the first year. Halya looked at everything and said she felt bad that she had not even started. Lynn pulled out a stack of diapers. "Here, this will get you started and here is how I have been making sleeper gowns. They are more of an open bag with a tie string at the bottom. Later, they can be used open as nightgowns."

"Oh thank you. I've been trying to think of where to start. My mind just seemed to go blank with too many things needing done. Now I have a starting point and maybe we can pool our supplies. I have a lot of soft sheets."

"I'm wondering if we should just stop with what we have now and then make as we need things?" Lynn asked.

"That probably would be a good idea, since I really don't know just what will be needed the most." Halya answered.

"Until we started going through these, I didn't realize just how many things I made. I guess they were going well and I just didn't stop. Maybe we should make a few more little blankets for just wrapping them in. They are going to need a lot until they get older since we have no plastic over pants to keep their clothes and bedding dry."

"This is going to be a learn-as-I-go experience for me." Halya said.

"I think we are both in the same boat on that one. I really never took care of babies before." Lynn replied.

Chapter 10

The next few weeks seemed to pass quickly. Everyone was busy during the shorter daylight hours and tried to keep outside noise to a minimum. The radio reports said the invaders were no longer around Fairbanks, so they took the chance to use the chainsaws and cut a lot of trees for future firewood and building projects. They tried not to clear cut in any area to be noticeable. They didn't know if anyone would ever see aerial photos of the area to compare the past with the present of not. They just didn't want to take too many chances.

James and Simon talked about going back to where they had been living, but didn't know whether or not they would have anything left to go back to. After a lot of evenings spent discussing it, they were invited to stay. They accepted. The more people they could depend on the better the chances of their survival. Gabe told them they were welcome to stay in the garage if they wanted. If the chance presented itself after break-up, they would dig out another place for them, if they wanted and to be looking around now for something they liked.

They found another area similar to Lynn's with a bit of a rock ledge and decided on following her building design. They started gathering building materials now as they fell fire wood trees. Poles were numerous in many areas and they cut them to length, then carried them home so they didn't leave too many wide trails all over the valley. Sooner or later, someone might fly over.

The radio report close to the New Year was slightly encouraging. There was a bit of information leaking out in the Lower 48 and they were calling for investigations into the reports. So far, nothing seemed to be coming from it, but word was getting out.

Both Lynn and Halya were now starting to show enough to notice. No one mentioned it and they worked at everything needing done. Neither one had gained much weight but they both were getting much thicker around the middle. They were still able to wear their regular clothes but the waists were tied across with soft rope.

The sound of a snowmobile put everyone on high alert. When Jesse pulled up, he held his hands out to the side to let them know it was a friendly visit. They still didn't recognize him until he pulled his helmet off. Then he laughed and apologized, "Sorry, I forgot this is a different machine than I used last time. That one needed some repairs so my brother traded with me, he is an excellent mechanic."

"How is Marilee and little James?" Lynn asked.

"Oh, they are doing great. I just wanted to drop off some furs we had on hand as a small thank you for all you did for us last time we were here. Our group is doing very well and we wanted to invite all of you to come out there, if you would like to be farther out of town."

"In some ways, I would like to be farther out, but in others, we are fairly well set up here and hope we can elude the invaders and manage to survive until they are gone and the State is back to normal or as normal as it is ever going to be, now that so many have been murdered. I wish we had a governor with some guts that would just declare us an independent nation. Since our own federal government has basically declared war on us that seems like a logical next step." Gabe said.

"I'm not sure we still have a governor and legislature." James put in. "There seems to have been quite a bit of invader activity in the Southeastern part of the State, from one of the broadcasts I heard."

"I heard something about that, too." Jesse added. "I hope I can spend the night and leave early in the morning for town. I was thinking without the invaders there, maybe some people might be back in town and maybe we could trade for stuff we would like to have."

Jesse went back to the toboggan he was pulling, took out a bundle of very nice beaver pelts and handed them to Halya. "Here you go. These make really great work hats and mitts. Probably make good boot uppers if you have moose hide or something to make soles out of."

They all went in the cabin and Lynn and Halya started an evening meal. They still had frozen moose steaks to thaw once in a while and this happened to be an evening they were making chicken fried moose steak again. Jesse swore he knew it when he left home and was the sole reason he was here. It was his favorite dinner ever since he had it here, last trip.

After dinner, everyone relaxed and checked to see if there would be a radio broadcast this evening. The windup radio worked well, but they didn't want to wear it out too soon. They were just glad it didn't require batteries. The windup lanterns and flashlights were really good, too. They got a lot of use. Lynn wished her headlamp was, she would run out of batteries soon and then be out of luck on finding more.

When the radio boomed out a broadcast, it startled them. It wasn't the usual one they listened to. The signal was very loud and clear. The voice sounded familiar and it was a little bit before Lynn recognized it. "That's Travis."

"Are you sure?"

"Yes, he used to stop and visit once in a while to see if I was doing okay. He worried about me living there alone." Lynn answered.

"I'm only going to repeat this one more time tonight. The invaders are headed back toward Fairbanks by train. They are supposed to be arriving day after tomorrow night, late, but don't count on them following a schedule. There is also supposed to be a heavy storm warning going into effect tomorrow evening. Anyone out and about, be sure and be inside before it hits. I'll try and get back on here within a few days to update on what we have found out. In the meantime, stay safe and warm. Keep your powder dry."

"Hmm, wonder if I should just try to get as far as possible tonight, then on in, in the morning and look around and right back out?"

"Are you sure you still want to go on in?" Simon asked.

"Yes, the storm will cover my tracks and it might be the only time I can even try. Anyone want to ride along?" Jesse replied.

Lynn actually wanted to go. Before she said anything though, Simon spoke up. "I would. Dad, may I?"

"If Jesse is going, he needs someone to watch his back and you are the best person I know for that." James answered. "I don't think it is really wise to go, but if you both want to, probably better get suited up and on your way."

"How are you doing on gas?" Lynn asked.

"I have enough to get there and back and even on home but if you can spare any, I would like to pick it up on my way home. I will leave my empties here that I filled the tanks with as soon as I got here."

Jesse and Simon were soon on their way toward Fairbanks. Everyone hoped they were not headed into trouble or bringing trouble behind them when they returned.

"Well, we know Travis is still okay, anyway." Lynn said as they went back in the house. "I have been worried about him and Rich."

As soon as it was light enough to work outside, they filled the gas cans left behind by Jesse so they would be ready when he stopped on his way home. Then they made busy work, worrying about the two in town. Just after dark, they heard the whine of a snowmachine coming up the valley. They faded into the trees and surrounding cover until they were sure of who was coming.

"Whooee, come out, come out, wherever you are, it's just us." Jesse called out as he pulled into the yard. "Those folks in town were sure happy to see us and we made a score on supplies. No food, they are low on food, but we got baby stuff and materials, building supplies like nails and spikes. I told them about the radio broadcast we heard and they are planning a little surprise for the invaders if they come back in tonight or tomorrow or any time in the future. There aren't many folks in town but they are really well armed. One man said he could get the National Guards back in and the Militia. So we are looked at as heroes for letting them know."

Simon was smiling as he climbed off the back of the snowmachine and they opened up the cover over the toboggan. They lifted out some bolts of fleece cloth, a bag of baby clothes and a few boxes of nails and spikes. There were some mukluks that were military issue and some boxes of miscellaneous tools. They filled the snowmachine up and then put the filled cans belonging to Jesse in the load and lashed the cover back on tightly. He waved goodbye and headed for home.

"That was quite an experience," Simon said as they carried the bolts of material into the cabin. "When Jesse says he is making a quick trip, he really means it. I didn't know a stock snowmobile could travel that fast. The folks in town were happy to see friendly faces and to know there are still some of us alive out here. They were not inclined to be friendly at first, but Jesse soon had them believing him. I think he could talk his way out of anything."

As they went inside, the front edge of the storm started moving in from the south. It seemed to be moving slower than Jesse was, so they hoped he beat it home.

The days were getting longer now, but only by a few minutes a day. It did make a difference and they were all looking forward to summer in some ways. They didn't know whether or not the 'peacekeepers' were going to increase their presence here or not. The uncertainty didn't help their nerves and they found themselves snapping at each other over trifles.

Then they heard another radio report on the results of the intruders return to Fairbanks. With the advance notice, the Guards and Militia set up a surprise welcome for them down the tracks quite a ways from town. They blew out a large culvert then set the charges to blow another one behind the train as soon as it passed, so it couldn't just back up and escape.

It worked beyond their wildest dreams. The train was speeding when it hit the ruined culvert and derailed badly. The Engineer was driving blind through the storm and didn't see the track missing at all. The explosion behind the train wouldn't have been needed, but was spectacular. That train was not going anywhere.

As usual, the invaders were not dressed for the weather conditions and as they poured out of the train, the Guard and Militia members opened fire then faded away into the storm.

The surviving invaders tried hiking on to Fairbanks but most died from the weather. There were bodies spread all along the tracks. After the storm cleared, the Militia went back and salvaged all the weapons from the baggage cars and the food supplies, also. They did a distribution in Fairbanks which eased the food and weapon shortage there. Now everyone was supplied with a good weapon and plenty of ammo, also. Anyone wearing a blue helmet or their uniform were fair game. It was not a good time to use salvaged clothing from the invaders.

Lynn and Halya made a special treat to celebrate. Real eggs were a distant memory, but they were well supplied with powdered eggs, even though they used them sparingly. Who knew when they could replace them? They used some of their flour and sugar and made a cake. Between the news and the treat, spirits were much better over the next several days and they tried to make sure everyone spent at least part of each day outside. That seemed to keep the cabin fever symptoms at bay.

Both women were now definitely showing signs of the population increase due in a little while. James was completely recovered from his injuries and able to help out more on the firewood getting. He and Simon already had a good supply of building poles stacked where they wanted to build. Once the ground was thawed, that project should not take much time.

Chapter 11

The sound of an airplane sent everyone inside. It was very high and probably could not have seen them, even if they stood outside and waved flags. But they were taking no chances. They waited quite a while after it was gone before edging back outside. A few days later, they heard another one. This one was going back. Later, they heard disturbing news on the radio.

An investigation had been called for into the handling of Alaska and a group of people from Congress came up to see for themselves. They had all been killed just after landing in Anchorage and the blame placed on the rebel Alaskans. Of course no Alaskans could get anywhere near the airport, but that little fact wasn't mentioned.

Now there was public outrage in the Lower 48 against those terrible Alaskans. The media was making a circus out of it. The tame photographer that filmed the massacre never questioned why he and his camera were left alone. The hysterical reporter seemed to assume the media would never be harmed. The masked armed intruders at the airport met no resistance whatsoever from any of the 'peacekeepers' stationed all around the airport. It was so cheesy and staged that Lynn wondered how any adult could possibly believe it. Everyone just focused on the dead Congressmen and women.

Now the President was calling for the military to invade. No one seemed to even question the entire action. Had people in the Lower 48 become so accustomed to this wannabe king that they just went along with anything he said? Lynn tried seeing it from the perspective they had been given and started to understand a little bit of their way of thinking.

Everyone down there "Knew" Alaskans were weird and different. They had to be, to live in those conditions on purpose. Yes, Alaska was a beautiful vacation destination, but people could be hired to travel up to take care of tourists. Just make the entire State into a huge Park and run it as such. They could even have theme areas. Native villages to stare at and wonder how they used to survive. Since they didn't have to do that anymore, they should be happy to get moved to a better location. Why wouldn't they be happy to get to live on a nice Reservation in a warm desert?

When Lynn told the group all this at dinner that evening, everyone started to laugh, then stopped and thought about it. She did have a point there. The animal rights groups and the wilderness worshippers would embrace a people free Alaska. As long as they were allowed to be there when they wanted, of course. Just like the head of a well-known environmental group that got an area designated as Wilderness, then flew his entire wedding party in by helicopter to hold his wedding where no one could ever go with a motorized vehicle, completely ignoring the fact that he had just broke the very Law he had fought to get passed. He was horrified when someone dared mention that little item to him. HE was not a lawbreaker. HE was celebrating a victory and his wedding with his very good friends. No law breaking there. A helicopter was different than an airplane or ATV. Well, no, they're not.

Just what could be done to rectify this new danger threatening them? No one could think of a single thing that could or would help them. It was depressing.

They were subdued for several days, but work continued around the place. James managed to go up to Lynn's house, go in the back window and disarm the bomb on the door long enough to take her rocking chair and a spare bed out. Then he rearmed the bomb and swept away most of the tracks before bringing the items down to her.

She was so happy to have a real mattress on her bed that she had tears in her eyes, then he said the chair was so she could rock her little one when it arrived. Then the tears fell. She wiped them off her cheek and thanked him. That was the nicest thing anyone had ever done for her.

Then he handed her the bag of candy bars he found stashed behind the bed.

"Oh wow, how did I ever forget them? How is that for not thinking, I hide my stash so well I even forgot it." she laughed.

He didn't want to sound nosey, but curiosity was eating him alive. Here she was, obviously alone, going to have a baby in a couple of months and no father in sight or ever mentioned by anyone.

"You can tell me to mind my own business if you want, but I would like to know about the baby." he said.

"Oh, I figured maybe Gabe or Halya mentioned that already. We took a prisoner, he got loose, broke into the garage where I was staying and they got him before he killed me. He had already been in there a little while though. He knocked me out, so I don't know exactly what happened but a few weeks later I started the morning sickness and dizziness and now you see the rest of the story."

"You seem so calm about the baby."

"Not it's fault. He will never have a part of its life, nor anyone else's. It's too bad it happened, but I will never blame the baby. It is all mine." her arms cradled her growing stomach.

He decided it would be a stupid person that tried to get between her and her young. He smiled at her and told her the baby would be lucky to have her for its mother.

"I don't know about that. Halya and I have no actual knowledge on child care. These babies are going to be a learning experience for both of us. She grew up in the Mideast and baby girls are not cherished there. I grew up in foster homes, not exactly models of loving kindness for the most part."

"Well, if I am around, maybe I can help out. My wife died when Simon was very young and I had always helped her out as she was never in good health. So I do have some experience with little ones."

"Thank you, James. That is an offer you may be sorry you ever made." she smiled up at him.

"Somehow I doubt that. I look at you and see a very strong capable young woman. Just looking over your home up the hill showed that you are extremely capable. Somehow, I don't think you had much help or ran to someone else every time you needed something done." he smiled back at her.

Halya decided her house needed a thorough cleaning, so they started in on it. Everything was moved and cleaned. They thawed enough snow to wash all the laundry needing done. They were both worn out by evening but the house was clean. The moose roast in the oven smelled delicious and they added rice, dried onions and celery to the broth in the pan about an hour before time to eat. Then they both plopped down on the couch and relaxed for the first time that day.

After a while, Halya asked Lynn what labor felt like.

"I don't know. They call them contractions, or labor pains, but no one has ever said exactly what that is supposed to feel like."

"I've felt odd all day today. Not bad or painful, just odd. But now I need the bathroom and right now." as she sprinted for the bathroom. "Oh, wow."

Lynn struggled upright and headed toward the bathroom to see if Halya was okay.

"Lynn? Would you call Gabe in, please?"

"Sure, anything I can do for you before I go?"

"Could you bring me a towel?"

"Here, I'll be right back." Lynn hurried to the door.

Lynn opened the door and started to yell for Gabe, thought better of it and walked out to find him. Just because it had been a while since anyone was around didn't mean she could just yell.

She found him with James and Simon in the Garage, told him Halya wanted him and hurried back to the house.

When she walked in, Halya had the cot set up by the heater, the box of soft towels handy and the drawer they had used for little James nearby.

"So what DO the pains feel like?" she asked Halya.

"I feel like I ate something that didn't agree with me, except it isn't steady. It hits, feels uncomfortable for a while, then eases off and goes away. I would still think something I ate was the problem, except my water broke while I was in the bathroom. I'm pretty sure that means I'm actually in labor, don't you?" she smiled mischievously.

"Yes, I'd say you probably are. At least now I will know what to look for, when it is my turn." Lynn answered.

"At least we both know what to expect after Marilee had little James here. I had no idea, before that."

"True. That was a pretty graphic demonstration." They both laughed.

Gabe hesitantly entered the room. "Are you at the 'give me the ax' stage yet?"

"Not yet, Gabe. I'm already prepared, anyway, after listening to Marilee." she held up a small sharp hatchet.

"Aww, Honey, really?" he grimaced.

She put the hatchet back by the heater where she used it to cut small kindling when the fire was out.

"Not really, Sweetheart. I just couldn't resist." She started laughing but cut it off short as a stronger contraction hit.

After it passed, she walked over to the cot. "I think I better get ready, I think your son is ready to meet his father."

"Oh? You know it is a boy now? All this time it has been IT and now it is SON?"

"I just have a feeling, besides, you are getting older and need a son to help you in your old age."

"Woman, if you weren't in the process of giving birth, I think I would have to paddle your behind. Me? Old? I'm not even 30 yet."

"Ha, just try that, even now you couldn't paddle me. You know what would happen to you if you did." and she smiled showing all her teeth.

He flinched. "Yes Dear."

They hugged through her next contraction, then he helped her lay down on the cot. "Don't you have too many clothes on for this?" he asked.

Lynn was in the kitchen, again putting a pot of water on to boil.

"I know, it is just something to get people out of the way. In stories and the movies it seems needed. In real life, not so much, but we do need sterile water to wash in and to clean up later. Plus sterilizing the string to tie the cord with. Besides, someone says a baby is being born, I start water boiling. It's getting to be a habit." she grinned at them both.

They started laughing just to be cut short as a strong urge to push hit Halya. "Okay, I actually do have too many clothes on."

She peeled off her PJ bottoms and settled back on the pad of towels on the cot. Then Gabe draped the sheet over her to cover her up. Then he went out to bring in another armload of firewood.

Halya hissed, "Lynn."

Lynn was still drying her hands but rushed over to see what was needed. Halya grabbed her hands and held on tightly while a major contraction passed. The next one hit immediately and Halya gasped. Lynn peeked under the sheet and made a grab as the baby made its appearance during a third strong pushing contraction.

She placed the baby on Halya's stomach and found the towel ready on the table beside her. She covered the baby and finished sterilizing the string. As soon as the cord quit pulsing, she tied it off and cut it, then wrapped the baby securely in a warm towel.

"Well, a boy or a girl?" Halya asked.

"Oops, didn't check."

Gabe came in the door as they unwrapped the baby to check. "Wow, it IS a boy." he exclaimed.

"Shut the door. He doesn't need to start out getting frostbite." Halya yelled.

Gabe hurried on in with the wood and washed up. Then he came over to Halya and sat on the stool beside the cot. He hugged her and the baby to him. "I've been so worried, afraid something would need a doctor or some kind of medicine or something. Are you okay? Really, really okay?"

"Yes, I am okay and so is your son. He even has all his fingers and toes. Two eyes, a nose and a mouth, even. He is perfect."

"Of course he is. You are such a perfectionist." Gabe told her.

Chapter 12

Gabe went out to tell the others he had a son. Lynn helped Halya get cleaned up and settled better on the cot with plenty of pillows behind her to sit upright.

By the time the other three trooped in, Halya was sitting up against the cushions holding her son. The little fleece cap they had made, on his head and firmly wrapped in a large warm towel.

Lynn brought her a cup of the broth they had on hand from the moose bones. Then she started dinner. Halya sipped at the broth then suddenly laughed and said she really wanted a steak.

"You are in luck. That's what you are getting to celebrate the birth of your son. He can't have any yet, but soon you will be mashing up meat for him." Lynn told her.

"I think I will start on something more like oatmeal. I think babies are supposed to be fed bland foods, aren't they?"

"I haven't a clue, Halya. I just figure as soon as milk isn't enough, I will slowly start adding in the foods I eat." Lynn answered.

"Sounds like a good plan to me." Halya answered.

Lynn cleaned up the kitchen after dinner. The men had been working on preliminary building on James and Simon's house. They were lashing sections of poles together so that once the ground was prepared, they could set up the walls and get the roof over it in a matter of a few hours.

When she got home she brought in enough wood to replace what she had used the last few days. She still preferred to keep everything well stocked. The daylight hours were now long enough there was no need for a light, as long as she didn't stay up all night. So after she finished the firewood, she cleaned up around indoors.

When the water was hot on the small fire she lit to take the chill off the house, she bathed and washed out what little bit of laundry she had ready. By the time she went to bed, even the honey bucket was clean. The large clean barrel behind the stove was full of clean snow, melting for water.

Dinner hadn't settled too well and she finally gave up trying to sleep and sat near the window and read a book. The baby had been turning somersaults earlier in the day but finally settled down and seemed to be sleeping, whether she could, or not. There was no way to get comfortable. She finally dozed off and on but still couldn't find a position that something wasn't gouging or poking her the wrong way.

She finally put on some heavy clothes and went outside. The night was just dark enough to see the aurora dancing directly overhead, so she leaned back against a snowbank and watched it. The beauty of it dancing overhead took her mind off the discomfort of her tummy and she relaxed. The shifting dancing colors almost hypnotized her and she gazed at it in awe. She had seen some fantastic displays before, but this one was outstanding.

The air was so still she felt like everything was watching this display with her. Not a whisper of a breeze moved through the night. Not a sound of a motor anywhere to disturb it. No lights to compete with the awesome lights dancing away in the sky. With her winter gear on, she could stay here as long as she liked in complete comfort, so she settled into the snowbank and just enjoyed watching. Even her upset stomach receded into the back of her mind.

At first the dampness intruded as the possibility that her overstressed bladder had relieved itself without her paying attention which embarrassed her badly. She hadn't done anything like that since she was about 2 years old.

Then she decided oh well, she was already a mess, she might as well continue to watch the sky and go in when the display ended. She still had water heating on the stove and she could wash herself and the clothes then. Abruptly, she really had to get to the bathroom, her tummy distress was now something she could not ignore. She gazed once more at the display of lights and was pleased to see they were slowly fading away. She had got to see the truly amazing part of this evening's display as a private show, just for herself.

By now, her need was urgent and she barely got the door closed and her pants down, before she found that her real problem was that her child was in the process of being born. She hobbled over to the stool by the stove and knelt down beside it, bracing her hands on the stool. She grabbed the towels she had used earlier in the evening for her hair and pushed them down between her knees on the floor.

A sudden strong urge to push gripped her and she went with it. Her child slid out onto the pile of towels and she held the stool with one hand while wrapping a towel over the baby with her other hand. Where was a string when you need one, she thought. Then she pulled the string from her boot. Not exactly sterile, but nothing she could do about that now.

As soon as she could manage it, she pulled off her outdoor clothes and grabbed a blanket from the end of the cot she used as a couch. When she picked up the baby, it opened its eyes and gazed at her. She gazed back.

With the baby cradled in one arm, she finally found the lamp and got it lit. Then she looked around for her box of medical supplies. The small bottle of antiseptic was in the bottom, of course. Once she got it open, she dabbed the umbilical cord and shoe string liberally with it. Then she looked the baby over and found herself smiling at the small wrapped bundle. She had a lovely little daughter.

The mess in front of the stove could be cleaned up in the morning, she needed some sleep. She did wad up the towels and contents and put it all in a box near the door.

She didn't have a drawer handy to use as a baby bed. She did have diapers though, so put one on the tiny body. Then one of the sleeper gowns and a small hat on her head to help keep her warm.

The cats came over to look over this small newcomer and curled next to her on the bed. Lynn curled on the other side and soon they were all asleep.

She woke up a couple of hours later to a small mewing sound that was her daughter. The cats looked at her in surprise, then snuggled back down asleep and left it to Lynn to take care of. Lynn knew she wouldn't have actual milk yet, but still put the baby to nurse. They both went back to sleep. A few hours later, Lynn woke up to the sounds of the men out near the garage. Usually she couldn't hear them through the thick walls. What was happening?

She tucked the baby into a blanket pouch she had made for carrying her after she pulled on some clothes and the baby. She stuck her handgun into the pouch with the baby and the small hand ax into the blanket she draped over her shoulder like a poncho.

She eased around the snow drift at the corner of her house and saw a stranger holding a gun on James and Simon. She didn't even think about it. She smacked him in the back of the head with the hand ax. He went down like a sack of potatoes. James jumped on him and Simon grabbed his weapon.

"Oops, meant to use the other side. Did I kill him?" she asked.

"I think so. He was one of the ones stranded out the road late last winter but he does not look like he suffered any and somehow none of them survived the winter. Usually that means he followed the example of the Donner Party in the 1800's down in California." James said.

Simon looked at his Dad. James explained. "The survivor ate the rest of the party."

"Ewww, bet he was popular after that."

"I don't think anyone wanted to travel with him, anyway."

Lynn said "I better go check on Halya and Gabe. What if this one wasn't alone?"

"I'm pretty sure he was, from the way he talked, but yes, we should be checking on them instead of just standing here. By the way, thank you. You just saved our lives." James said.

They dragged the body over beside the trail to dispose of later. Then they proceeded carefully over to the main house. Gabe was just coming out the door as they reached it.

"Oh, sorry I'm late this morning. We were just admiring what a good job we do making babies." He laughed.

James told him they had an intruder over at the garage and he immediately sobered up. "We are getting complacent again. We are going to have to pay better attention. Come on in and we can decide what to do about him."

They went inside and Lynn went in to check on Halya. She found Halya just waking up. Halya reached over and picked up her little one and Lynn pulled back the poncho and removed the little pouch. It squeaked, Halya jumped and looked over in time to see Lynn uncovering a perfect little girl.

"What the…how..when..GABE." she yelled.

Gabe came barreling into the bedroom to pull up short with James and Simon right on his heels.

Lynn sat there holding her new daughter while everyone stood or sat there mouths open, just looking at her.

"You mean when you just came out and saved our lives, you also were carrying your newborn you just delivered yourself?" James blurted out.

"What was I supposed to do, let the man shoot you both?" Lynn asked.

"But how did you manage? When did you know you were in labor?" Halya asked.

"Actually, I didn't realize I was in labor until she was on her way out. I got sidetracked watching the most amazing aurora last night and ignored the contractions I guess. I may have been having them a while as my stomach has been a little upset the last couple of days."

"What are you going to name her?"

"Right now, I think Aurora. That aurora was so fantastic and it led me through the entire birth, practically. She was almost born out against the snowbank. If I had not been wearing pants, she probably would have been."

Everyone looked at her in amazement. "You mean you just stayed out there until she was almost born?" Halya asked.

"Yes, then I thought I had to use the honey bucket, that the cramps from something I ate was getting to me, then I thought my bladder sabotaged me, guess that was the water breaking. I was pretty disgusted with myself. All in all, I still had my boots on and pants around my ankles when she was born by the stove. One of my boot laces is still tied on her cord. I did use a lot of antiseptic on it later."

Halya had collapsed on the bed laughing. "I can just see it all now. Only you could manage something like that then save two guys as an afterthought."

Chapter 13

The men trooped back into the front room while Halya got dressed. Lynn sat on the edge of their bed, holding Aurora in her arms. She really hadn't had a chance to look her over really well. When she got dressed, she was in a hurry and just grabbed whatever was handy. It showed. She was wearing a pair of PJ bottoms, an oversized T shirt she used as a dust cloth and her winter boots missing one string. Her hair was not brushed, it was just covered with a hat jammed over it. Her coat did cover almost everything, but she looked a mess.

"Guys, I don't think I locked my door when I came out this morning. Would someone mind going back over with me and checking inside to make sure no one is in there? I would feel better about going back in with the baby." Lynn asked.

James and Simon both jumped up to go with her. James told her she probably wouldn't have rushed out if she didn't have to come rescue them. Halya asked if she was coming right back and she said she would be back in a bit, she wanted to change into real clothes and maybe even brush her hair. She pulled off her hat and Halya laughed, "Okay, see you after a while. That might take a bit to fix."

Lynn walked home a bit slower than she had rushed out this morning, earlier. James and Simon walked along with her and James stayed outside with her as Simon searched through her home to make sure no one was hiding in it. She felt silly for asking them, but now she was responsible for another human being and she had to be sure she was safe. It was amazing how protective she felt for this tiny person held against her chest.

Simon came out and said the place looked amazingly nice and neat. She blushed, thinking of all the cleaning she had done last night. She had not even thought of how Halya had cleaned before going into labor. As she thought it all over, she felt she was really in denial, thinking no, it just couldn't be possible.

They all walked in and she offered to make them some tea or hot chocolate, she still had a lot on hand. They declined and told her they should be taking care of her, she was the one that just gave birth.

She laughed and said it was actually easier than she had expected from things she had heard and seen before. She did credit zoning out watching the lights for relaxing her so much that she ignored the contractions. She looked around for somewhere to put the baby. She finally placed her on her cot/couch and put pillows on each side of her. For now, that would have to do.

Then she put a kettle on the stove to heat water and took her overcooked breakfast off. The men excused themselves and left. She ate her share of the breakfast rice and mixed up the rest for the cats. The box of towels was pulled over from behind the door and set to soak in the tub of melted snow. She should have done that last night, she thought. She hoped she could soak them clean. She wasn't sure how strong she was for scrubbing yet.

She found some clean clothes and got redressed. Then worked on her rats' nest of hair. It was long enough now she just braided it. She finally felt like she looked human again. She nursed the baby and changed her, then added her diapers into the soak water. She put some homemade laundry soap in it and using a plunger, gave the mess a few plunges to work the soap through. She left it all sit and locking the door, this time, she carried Aurora back over to Gabe and Halya's house.

When she got to the door, the men were just coming back out. Gabe held the door for her to walk on in and then closed it as they went over to the garage.

Halya was on the couch with their little boy.

"So, what are you going to name him?" she asked Halya.

"We really haven't settled on a name yet. Gabe don't want him to be called Junior and I can't say I blame him. I don't want to name him after my father as that would not be a popular name here and Gabe doesn't care for his father's name, Percival."

"Oh, I see his point. What is Gabe's middle name?"

"His actual name is Gabriel Joseph Halloran."

"Why not reverse them and name the boy Joseph Gabriel Halloran instead, that is what my Dad's family did. No Juniors that way." Lynn told her.

"Oh, we never thought of that and I will ask Gabe what he thinks of it."

Lynn noticed the baby was being called Joseph before Gabe ever came back in the house.

About three days after Aurora was born, while Lynn was busy hanging up the laundry she had just washed, her milk came in with a vengeance. She felt like she suddenly had two gallon bottles hanging on her chest. She truly hoped Aurora was really hungry as she rushed over the pick her up. Aurora was only too happy to oblige. Finally, real milk.

Lynn and Halya both had to laugh about the changes in their shapes. Halya had always been small and rather slender. Now she was small but voluptuous. Gabe couldn't keep his eyes off her. Lynn was much taller and looked more like a Norse goddess of old. Now that her hair had grown out so much and she was wearing it braided over her head, maybe a Valkyrie. When she insisted on helping with the outdoor work, she wore the baby in a sling pouch she made and the baby didn't even show.

They were on their way back to the houses when they heard the sound of an aircraft. They all scrambled under cover of the closest trees. Intent on staying out of sight. They all pulled their white parka covers up over themselves so they were completely covered in case it was low enough to see them.

After the plane was gone, Lynn realized something was on her parka cover. "Watch out, they sprayed something and it is on our outer parka covers. Remember what we were told. We have to take these off and leave them outside when we go in the houses. Find something in your pockets to breathe through, if possible."

Aurora was underneath Lynn's parka and cover, but she was still worried about the baby. She kept the white cover pulled far over her head and her head down, so nothing falling from the sky could hit her skin.

As they hurried towards home, they agreed to stay indoors the next several days and listen for more planes overhead but also to see what the effects of this spraying would be.

As soon as she reached the overhang of the entryway of her home, she was pulling the cover off over her head to hang on the hook outside by the door. Her gloves and boots stayed outside, also. Inside, she pulled off the parka and insulated pants. Her hat joined them in a pile near the door. She opened up the heater and piled more wood in as she was shaking. That was probably as much from fear as from cold, but she felt chilled to the bone. She checked on Aurora and she looked okay, but she still gave her a warm bath to wash any possible contamination from her, then followed suit by washing her hair and herself, also. She was glad she had a lot of snow melt water on hand and a large pot of it on the heater at all times.

Lynn didn't feel very good the next morning. She didn't know if it was from worry and nerves or from what they had been sprayed with. She remembered hearing about the government releasing some viruses in the subway system of New York City just to see what the results would be. Would they actually spray something lethal on their own people? Since the trees were not leafed out yet and there was still snow on the ground, she couldn't tell if it was something like Agent Orange that would exfoliate all plant growth and cause untold misery to people for years to come. The last time she felt like she was coming down with something, she gave birth. What would this time bring?

Then she thought of the evergreens. If it was against plant life, surely it would ruin them and show up within days. She opened her door long enough to check the foliage of the spruce closest to the house and to remember details for the next time she checked.

Lynn still didn't feel very good the next day. She couldn't pinpoint exactly what was wrong, it was just a feeling of malaise. From listening to friends when she was a teenager, it felt like their descriptions of a giant hangover. Her head ached and she felt bad all over, even her bones ached. The baby was fussier than usual as she was a good natured baby and usually didn't fuss at all. If this was from whatever they were sprayed with, she would personally like to handle the health care of the person responsible.

She spent the next few days designing assorted tortures to inflict on her unknown instigator. He, she or it, they would pay.

The spruce trees didn't appear harmed, so she thought at least they had not been sprayed with Agent Orange. She thought maybe it was something similar to the toxic perfluorocarbons used in the New York subway system. They had declared the gas to be safe. However, the people handling it were suited up in full contamination suits with respirators. If it was so safe, why didn't they handle it like water without the suits?

That gas was a waste product from aluminum processing and everyone knows how safe that all is. Even the Nazis used fluoride in concentration camps to keep the inmates docile. Was this spraying program devised to make whatever remained of the population docile for the upcoming summer? Well, she doubted it would do her much good. She never did follow the herd.

After a week, she was done with staying indoors. The snow pack was mostly gone and the small river had water running over the ice on it. She still covered herself and the baby with the winter gear and when she got outdoors, she pulled the cover on over the whole works, including over her head. Then reversed the process when she reached Gabe and Halya's. She brought along a batch of cookies she made one evening when she began to get a little stir crazy from being cooped up in the house so long without going outside.

Gabe and Halya were happy to see her. They had been feeling about the same as she had, although Halya didn't start until the day after Gabe, so was probably from handling his clothing or something. They all still felt a little lethargic but hoped that would wear off once they could get back outdoors and back to work.

About the time Lynn thought she should go home, James and Simon came over. So she sat back down, ate another cookie and everyone discussed the recent spraying they had received. Both men were just now feeling recovered enough to resume some work. Like the rest, they felt slowed down and tired easily.

When Lynn told them how she had spent her time designing tortures for the person responsible for their discomfort, she made everyone laugh.

"Yes! I will help you." Halya exclaimed.

They heard the sound of a snowmobile coming and rushed to get geared up and stationed in the trees on the other side of the yard. They did not want to be caught with everyone in one location.

By the time the recognized Jesse, they knew something was wrong. He looked terrible. He was slender before, now he looked emaciated.

He had to try twice to get off the snowmachine and then Simon steadied him with a hand on his arm and his arm around his shoulder.

"What's wrong, what happened?" chorused in the yard as they helped him into the house.

"The dirty SOBs sprayed us with something. We were working outside and headed for the house but we all got covered in the spray. Do you have anything at all that helps get over whatever this is? Marilee is really bad. Little James is sick, but not as bad as Marilee. I'm afraid hers is going into pneumonia. I'm not too hot myself, but I just had to come see if there was anything to be done to help." Jesse looked so bad they wondered how he had managed to stay on the snowmachine for the trip here.

Lynn thought of the fishmox she had in her medicine kit and offered it. If Marilee had pneumonia, she needed antibiotics. It wasn't much but certainly better than nothing at all. She offered it to Jesse and he looked like he was going to kiss her or something.

"I hate to rush you, but she is really bad and I need to get right back to her. Is there anything else I can do to help her?"

Lynn went back over to her house while James offered to return with Jesse and help tend to the chores needing done as well as the medical needs. Jesse needed some recuperation time, also, from the looks of him. Jesse accepted and James hurried to pack. Gabe and Simon again topped off Jesse's gas tank. Halya and Lynn then packed some extra jerky and dried fruit they had on hand for the men to take back with them. The trip was going to be rough since it was about half snow and half dirt now on the hilltops they would be traveling.

Chapter 14

The two men left as soon as James was ready and Jesse had a bowl of soup. The soup seemed to revive him a bit and he thanked Halya for it and the large jug of it that she was sending home with him. The men wrapped it carefully and stuck it in between them on the snowmachine seat. It was warmth against Jesse's back and James' belly, but the day was not hot so it felt pretty good.

Marilee was not able to nurse little James very much so Lynn sent a bag of instant milk and a jar of molasses to add to it when it was mixed as a supplement for the baby. They had a couple of baby bottles so that might work if he would accept it.

After they left, Lynn felt slightly depressed that James wasn't there. Since she seldom spoke to him or even worked with him, she couldn't understand why she felt this way. He was a quiet thoughtful man and never pushed himself out to take credit for things, even when he was the originator of the idea. She actually missed him.

Everyone was feeling much better so they were trying to get stocked up on firewood and find some water that wasn't possibly contaminated by whatever had been sprayed on them. They were afraid to use the snow as they had been all winter. Did the stuff penetrate down into the snow? Was it a scum on the top of the snow? They were rationing the use of water to the essentials. Making sure everyone remained hydrated and washing out baby diapers. No showers, just wash downs with a damp wash cloth. The overflow water running on the frozen river was suspect also as it would possibly carry snow melt that was contaminated.

Lynn and Halya used some dirt they kept stored in buckets over the winter to start some plants for a garden of some sort later after the snow was gone. Not knowing what some of the seed pods Lynn brought down from her garden had been from was going to make this interesting. The tomato seeds were easy.

Simon came home late one evening with a box he was carrying very carefully. He went into the garage with it and carefully opened it. Inside were three of the sorriest looking chickens Lynn had ever seen. Their combs and wattles were mostly gone from freezing and they did not look happy to be confined to the box. Halya looked at Simon like he had just done the most wonderful thing possible.

"Chickens. Maybe we can have some eggs, real eggs, not the powdered stuff from a can. How can we keep them alive and happy?" she asked.

"These seem to be able to fly a bit, so I think first off, we need to clip the feathers on one wing to keep them earthbound. I'm not sure what to do about his crowing. That was how I found them to start with." Simon told her.

"If we get some eggs, maybe we should save the first ones and see if one of the hens gets broody and we can raise some chicks." Lynn suggested.

"Can we do that?" Halya asked.

"Yes, just don't let the eggs get too cold, maybe build a nest box when we fix them an area and hope they lay in the boxes. We need to find some gravel for them, also. I am amazed they made the winter." Lynn told her.

"I think these are the ones that lay colored eggs. They are from wild birds in South America and pretty hardy chickens. Araucanas or something like that." Simon put in.

Gabe and Simon immediately started building some sort of coop to keep the chickens in. The women had been quite vocal about missing fresh eggs and if the men were honest about it, they really missed them, too. Powdered eggs were fine for a lot of things, but they really missed having a fried or boiled egg now and then. It would be quite a while before they actually got to have a fried egg, even now, if they wanted to try increasing the little flock.

The men built a coop and cage on the other side of the backhoe in the garage. It would be warm but put some distance between the chickens and the men living in the garage. When the chickens were released into the new coop, they sat huddled together a bit before slowly venturing out to look their new domain over. Then the rooster climbed to the highest perch and crowed a rather rusty sounding little crow. Simon listened and said, "That is not the crow I heard over in the woods, maybe there are more chickens that survived the winter. I'll have to go back and look the area over better."

"Dinner is ready, so maybe you want to wait and go look another day?" Halya asked.

"If I go back over, I want to take a long handled net to catch them with. I found a short handled net hanging on one of the buildings there, and used it, but it wasn't easy."

"I'll go over with you, maybe two of us can corner them easier, if there are more left. Maybe we can increase the flock faster than we thought." Gabe offered.

"I am just amazed any made the winter, being on their own. These are really tough little chickens." Lynn said.

She brought over some of the gravel she kept at her house to mix with cat litter for the cat box. When she sprinkled some in the little coop, the chickens happily started pecking at it. "They are probably really needing that, by now." she said.

"I looked around really well to make sure there wasn't still someone living over there. I didn't want to take anything if there was any chance anyone was still alive in the area." Simon told them. "Should we check all the homes to see if anyone at all is around? If not, then maybe we should try to salvage anything we can use instead of leaving it for the invaders to use."

"I've been thinking maybe we should do that, too." Gabe replied. "I would hate to help the invaders in any way, so I have no problem coming along and we can do it better and faster if there are two of us."

After dinner, they planned on what they should take with them and would go back the next morning, fairly early.

Lynn offered the use of her akio and the pet carrier she had used to bring the cats down from the house in. They fastened it in with a small cargo net she used on the pickup bed. A small tarp would hold items from falling off as easily if they found things to bring home.

After Gabe and Simon left, Lynn and Halya started a house cleaning frenzy. First they did Gabe and Halya's house. Usually there were always guys around and even though they helped and sometimes got in the way, it was not quite the same as cleaning without anyone around. When they were done the place looked wonderful. They left a pot of soup on the stove and bread raising on the counter when they went over to Lynn's to clean.

Her house didn't take long as she had actually done a pretty thorough clean while waiting out the time after they got sprayed. Now their problem was finding enough clean water to keep the laundry done and still have water for food and drinking. Lynn had a small hand pump type water purifier, but she didn't know if it would remove whatever they were sprayed with.

The bread was just coming out of the oven when the men returned from their excursion. From the sounds, they had found more chickens.

There were two more hens in the pet carrier. The men said there were more chickens over there, if they could find some way to trap them without hurting them. Lynn suggested taking some gravel over and spreading it in a small area, then covering the area with a net. Even if they didn't catch any more, the gravel might help the remaining chickens survive until they could get gravel on their own when all the snow was gone.

The rest of the akio was loaded with flour, sugar and cooking oil. Gabe said there was a lot more food left, but he wanted to get all of this before someone else got to it. They had searched every building and saw no evidence of anyone still alive in that whole small community.

Halya was happy to see the baking supplies. She was even happier when she found the small box of spices on the bottom of the load.

Lynn spotted the boxes of ammunition under some bags of flour. There were a couple of calibers that she was not familiar with but she knew they had guns the rest would fit. If nothing else, she could carefully open and reuse the components by reloading into other shells.

The men had cushioned the load with a couple of lovely quilts and Lynn and Halya immediately grabbed them when they were uncovered.

"These are beautiful, guys, thanks for bringing them." Lynn said.

Simon looked sheepishly at her, "I only grabbed them to make the load more stable and not shift around so much on the way down the hill. There are a lot more quilts, blankets and sheets up there. Should we go get more stuff?"

"If you think you can, safely, then yes. I would go, but not sure what kind of load I could drag back, with Aurora." Lynn answered.

"I think right now is the safest we are going to be, just before breakup and new troops coming back in to subdue us. If we are going to get more of the stuff from up the hill, we better be packing as many loads a day as we can manage." Gabe said.

Gabe whistled as he looked around his home. "Wow, you were busy today, this is beautiful."

Halya blushed and told him "Thanks. I had help. Lynn and I cleaned houses today."

They clipped a wing on each of the new hens and placed them in with the other three chickens and Lynn swore the little rooster preened in front of his growing flock of ladies.

The men were up early the next morning and ate a quick breakfast. Halya packed a lunch although they planned on being back with a load before lunch. They took it with them, as her lunches were always good and they could eat it as a snack while they worked and still get lunch when they got back.

Lynn found an area under some trees that was free of snow. She wasn't sure why, but thought it might have a warm spring fairly close under the surface. It was just across the river from her house and downstream a very short distance. She hung Aurora in her little carry bag from a limb while she worked clearing the brush and moss from the whole area. The soil wasn't frozen under the moss, so she was pretty sure her thoughts about it were correct.

She was back at the house before noon, just as the men were coming into the yard with their loaded akio and backpacks. They had caught one more hen, but the others were getting very skittish now and stayed hidden when they came around. It looked like maybe there were quite a few more still up there. Maybe they could find some during the summer, if they were careful. This hen happened to be broody and would not leave her nest in one of the old sheds. So they brought nest, eggs and all. Sure enough, she was still on a nest inside the pet carrier. Well, this would really jump start their chicken supply.

The rice, noodles, mixes and box meals would be a welcome addition to their food supply. The piles of blankets and sheets could be made into clothing, besides being useful as bedding. Simon pulled out a bag of sewing thread from his backpack. Then a bag of buttons and another smaller bag of assorted needles and pins. These were true treasures.

The men made two more trips that afternoon. They had the supplies stockpiled away from the buildings and only needed to go that far to load up and come home.

Chapter 15

The supplies they managed to bring home were all things they would really be able to use. The last trip, Simon brought down a treadle sewing machine and gave it to Lynn. She immediately set it up and made him a jacket from a couple of the blankets.

The weather was too warm for his heavy duty winter parka. She put a hood on it that he could pull up over his head and a flap to cover most of his face for when the wind was blowing or he needed protection from any more spraying. Gabe liked it so much, she made one for him, also, then another to have for James, when he got back. She and Halya picked blankets they liked for theirs and she was working on them when she remembered her little cleared area across the river.

She asked the others to come with her to check it out.

When they all got there, everyone just stood and looked at the long narrow strip of ground that was totally thawed and free of snow. No one knew what to think about it so she explained what she thought it was. She had heard that there had been studies done all over the State on the hot springs and the ones considered warm springs. They might not actually be warm, just never froze up as the water was just warm enough to keep them above freezing, year around.

These springs were quite numerous over the entire State. About the only time they could be found was in winter. In rivers, they caused problems with winter travelers as sometimes they made open leads under the snowpack on top the river. This could be from where they entered the river from the side or actually came up under the riverbed and caused upwellings of warmer water under the ice.

Lynn said she was wondering if they could somehow pound down a well or at least build some sort of greenhouse over this spot. If they had a well point, and some pipe, they could possibly hit water before any enemy troops arrived to hear the pounding. If they could pound it in horizontally, the water would run on its own.

Gabe thought if he didn't have any, maybe there would be some, up the hill. Some of those places had been here long enough to have excellent junk piles out back.

"The soil looks pretty good here, also, so I think if we dig out the top soil, then cut the back area down level with the front. Build a solid back wall and roof, with a shed type roof, that it would be warmer from the water and the heat loss would be less when it starts to get colder. Maybe we could grow food most of the year, not just the usual three months we get now. If we could extend it a couple of months even, we could really increase our output of food." Lynn enthused.

Early the next morning, Lynn bundled up Aurora and took the akio up the hill to her place. She ignored the house and went directly to the supply of old 5 gallon buckets that she used for hauling rocks and dirt. They would work fine for the greenhouse.

She loaded all of them on the sled, then found a few more tools, shovels, hoes and grub hoes to add. By the time she started back down the hill, she had quite an impressive looking load. Since the buckets were all empty, it wasn't a heavy load. She finally made it to the site of the future greenhouse and parked the akio. Then she went on over to Gabe and Halya's.

They were just getting around as little Joseph was cranky during the night. Now he was sleeping peacefully and they were in no hurry. Lynn apologized and went home. Simon came down the hill from the other direction as she was leaving. She told him they weren't up yet and he laughed. He was returning from another trip to the old store. He pulled an old well point out of his backpack and a few lengths of pipe. "I came by to borrow your akio but you were already gone."

"Oh, if I had known, I would have left it for you. I went up for buckets and tools." she said.

"I think I found enough pipe. I heard that usually a horizontal well normally doesn't have to go very far for water." Simon told her.

"Have you had breakfast? We can talk over this project and eat." Lynn said.

"I can always eat and if this will improve our food supply, count me in for labor. I don't know how to grow things but I sure am willing to learn."

"The chickens improved our chances a lot and if we can get a safe source of water that will be another plus for us. Water warm enough not to freeze up in winter is a bonus. If we get a greenhouse over it all, we should do quite well indeed."

Lynn fixed them each a large sandwich of moose lunchmeat she mixed up. After changing the baby, they walked over to the greenhouse site. She hung Aurora back in the tree she usually hung her in while working here and started work. She was digging out from the uphill side, keeping the dark topsoil in buckets and once she passed it, the subsoil went to the downhill side.

Simon started in also and with the two of them working, they soon had a fairly level area dug out. There seemed to be a natural dip on the south side, so they decided to start attempting to pound in the pipe there. Lynn offered to hold the pipe and Simon countered by saying he could make a pipe holder that wouldn't say ouch and hit back every time he missed. He tied a couple of poles across to trees on either side and placed the well point across them. They positioned it exactly where they wanted and he drove a couple of short stakes in on either side to hold it in place. After a couple of whacks with the sledge hammer, he got it going in perfectly and soon was in a rhythm of pounding. The pipe went in easily enough and soon they added the next piece and put the cap back on to pound against.

Simon asked her to just put two pieces together and it would speed them up as the pieces were only five foot pieces. About forty feet into the project, he was sweating and Aurora wanted some attention, so they took a break. Lynn unscrewed the pounding cap and found it had some muddy water in it. No more came out, so they quit and headed over to the houses.

Gabe was on his way over to see just what they were doing when they reached the garage.

"We could hear you while still in the house. Just what were you two doing?"

"We are on our way to having water that no one can contaminate," Simon told him.

"Halya has dinner ready, so maybe we can all go see after we eat?"

"Dinner? We just had breakfast." Lynn said.

"Guess you missed lunch then." Gabe replied.

"It was going so well, we just never got to a place to stop. No wonder Aurora was wanting to come home." Simon told him.

"I gave her some of the ground up moose meat. She really likes it and it seems to fill her up better than just milk." Lynn told them. "Lasts longer between meals, too."

"Maybe we need to start doing that for little Joseph. He doesn't seem to be getting enough to eat lately." Gabe said.

"Halya, have you been taking the multi-vitamins?" Lynn asked.

"Yes, but since I've been sick, I don't seem to have enough milk to keep him happy."

"I know what you mean, I haven't, either. I think maybe we need to start supplementing their diets with ground meats and now we might start getting eggs once in a while. We should use an egg now and then for the babies. We can grow our flock a bit slower. The babies come first."

After dinner, they walked back over to see how the water project was doing and were surprised to see some muddy water drizzling out of the pipe. Lynn wanted to build some sort of deck from the greenhouse doorway out over the pipe after they got the greenhouse built. She and Simon had the floor down a couple of feet lower than the surrounding hillside and on the uphill side, about three feet deeper. She wanted to build the bottom solid on both sides and the ends and back wall totally solid. She thought if they used some of the white membrane roofing on the ceiling and back wall, the reflected light would improve the growing conditions in the greenhouse. Since they didn't have a lot of the greenhouse panels this would make the most of what they had. Lynn couldn't wait to get started.

Lynn carried her little bow saw with her whenever she walked in the woods, searching for small spruce to fall for the building. The water flow was steadily increasing from the pipe, and they had decided to leave it alone and see if it cleared up, also. Her pile of poles was steadily growing and soon she would start building on the walls.

Most of the snow was gone, except where drifts had left ridges of packed snow. Simon asked to borrow the akio for one last trip. She figured it was important or he would not be using it on the dirt.

When he returned, it was piled high, and she couldn't believe he managed to drag such an enormous load until she realized it was foam board. Even though the pile was taller than he was, it wasn't all that heavy.

They unloaded it into the garage. Gabe said if he had known the garage was going to be such a popular place, he would have made it even bigger than it was.

The next morning, they were just starting construction on the greenhouse when they heard someone walking through the brush and trees up the hill from them. They hunkered down and waited, being as quiet as possible when Aurora squeaked from being held a bit too tightly. Lynn immediately eased her grip, but now there was complete silence from the direction they had been listening to.

Lynn started sweating and realized she was also hyperventilating a bit. Simon was nowhere to be seen, having faded into the woods. Lynn eased her crouch down to being seated completely on the ground. Her legs were screaming in agony from how tense she had been holding them in the tight crouch. Her heart thundered in her ears and she was trying to blend her and Aurora into the tree she was leaning against when Simon spoke lowly, just behind her almost triggering the heart attack she felt ready to have.

"It's Dad and Jesse. They are headed on over to the house. They didn't see me yet."

Simon helped her stand up and then held onto her a bit as her legs still weren't too steady when they started walking quietly toward the house. She was happy to see both men looking pretty good when they came in sight. Jesse looked far better than he had when they left. James just looked his usual self.

They walked right in the door behind the two men and startled them both.

"So we DID hear something in the woods a little ways up the hill." Jesse exclaimed.

"I think you scared a few years off our lives," Simon told him.

"What were you two doing up on the hill over there?" James asked.

"Three, there were three of us." Lynn said as she uncovered Aurora and pulled her out of her pouch.

"Wow, she has certainly grown." James said.

Halya came out of the back room about then, holding little Joseph.

"Look at him, he is growing like a weed." James couldn't believe how much both little ones had grown. He knew he was gone longer than he planned but it certainly wasn't all that long.

Halya immediately asked Jesse how Marilee and little James were doing.

Jesse was beaming, so she figured it was good news. He said they were both doing very well and he needed to head back. He just wanted to make sure James got home in one piece and that they were all still doing okay. He asked if they heard the radio report a few nights back and they had to say they missed it.

"I don't know what that person in charge is thinking, but he has declared Alaska incorrigible and unable to govern itself and asked for more UN "Peacekeepers" to come in this summer and subdue us. China offered and Russia stepped in too, so no telling who all will be showing up now. He claims dissidents here have attacked and killed unarmed UN representatives and the entire delegation that came to investigate from Washington D.C. late last fall. You know, no matter what you call them, a rat by any other name is still a rat." Jesse shook his head. "I can't believe all the people in the Lower 48 actually believe what he is telling them."

James took up the narrative, "They are reporting huge food shortages all over in the Lower 48, so that is keeping most people's minds off our problems. I would be willing to bet, if I were a betting person, that Alaska will be used as an excuse for them to enforce Martial Law on the rest of the country. The elections have been cancelled."

Gabe had come in during the update and he immediately jumped in, "They what? How can they justify cancelling elections?"

"No one has to justify it if the Country is under Martial Law. They are starting a rationing system for food and fuel for vehicles. Texas has filed in Court to secede from the Union and most of the States that used to be part of Texas have filed to rejoin Texas. Well, I've certainly brightened up your morning, but I really do need to get headed back home. We need to work on camouflaging our homes better."

Jesse headed for the door and was soon on his way home. They had walked most of two nights to get here this morning. He was going to alternate jogging, then walking to speed up getting home. It was light all night now, so that would not be a problem. However, moving fairly fast, he would show up from a long distance away. He was afraid to leave Marilee and little James alone too long though.

Everyone had dozens of questions for James and he tried to answer everyone. Finally they noticed he was almost out on his feet, so finally let the man go get some rest.

Chapter 16

Simon and Lynn headed back to continue work on the greenhouse as it should already be planted and wasn't even built yet. The growing season is so short, even a few days could mean the difference between a nice crop and starvation. They did have a lot of seedlings growing in the houses to transplant as soon as possible.

They laid everything out that absolutely had to be nailed, then tried hammering in bursts, mimicking a woodpecker in the dead trees. It wasn't perfect, but they hoped no one was in hearing distance, anyway.

With the framework finished, they called it a day. The pipe was running about a third full of fairly clear water now, so Lynn took the little bucket she brought over back home, full of water. Simon took a drink and fell to the ground clutching his throat. Lynn about panicked until she saw the smirk on his face, then threw her bucket of water on him and refilled it.

James walked up the little slope about the time the water hit Simon. His laughter startled both of them and they stood there looking sheepish with Simon dripping water. It was so hard to remember the dangers every moment.

"I can see you two are working really hard." he said.

They each said "He/She started it." while pointing at the other one.

"Why do I feel like you two should be siblings? You act like you grew up together."

They smiled and stuck their tongues out at each other.

"Yeah, that's what I'm talking about. Such shining adult behavior in front of the little girl." James said.

Aurora stretched and yawned from her hanging cradle in the tree and blinked her beautiful green eyes at them. Lynn knew she only had moments before that sweet little rosebud mouth opened in piercing screams for food.

She unhooked the hanging pouch full of baby and headed for her house. As long as they were moving, it would remain quiet. She had a piece of jerky and handed that to her daughter to gum as she removed her outer gear and fixed the fire. Then she poured herself a cup of mint tea and sat down to nurse the baby.

She so didn't want to think about the problems that would arrive with summer. Thinking about what James and Jesse had told them this morning was enough to give her a headache. The next thing she knew, she heard a light tapping at her door. Aurora was done nursing, her tea was cold and she had a kink in her neck.

She gently placed the baby in her bed, fastened her clothes back together and checked the door. Halya smiled back at her.

She opened the door and Halya slipped inside, shutting the door behind herself.

"You missed dinner, I brought some over for you," Halya said, placing a plate on the table.

Lynn was rubbing her neck, "I guess I just slept through the whole evening. The last thing I remember was Aurora starting to nurse and me reaching for my tea."

"I think maybe you should take some time to relax and get some rest. Are you sleeping well or is Aurora waking you up every few hours?"

"She is usually sleeping through the night now, since I started added some solid food to her diet. So I think I'm getting enough sleep. I just want to get the greenhouse done, planted and a crop started for next winter's food." Lynn told her.

"Yes, I worry about food, too. We know we won't be able to restock this summer like we usually do, but we will restock with as much as we can." Halya answered. "Worry won't make it better or increase our supplies."

"I know, but it sure is easier to know something than it is to actually let it go and rely on the future just taking care of itself." Lynn told her.

The delicious odors from the plate on the table drew Lynn like a magnet. "You are such a good cook, Halya. I love the way you make everything so delicious."

"Thank you. You are easy to cook for, you never complain."

"What's to complain about? You fix wonderful meals. I can cook, but sometimes I just make oatmeal and that is my dinner. You always make something extra."

"Okay, finish eating. The guys want us all together while we discuss what we have to expect this summer. But thank you for enjoying my cooking. I like fixing good food, while we have it."

That sounded ominous, so Lynn finished eating, wrapped up Aurora and accompanied Halya back to their house.

Everyone else was still sitting around the table, talking, when they came in. The men stopped whatever they were talking about and waited for the women to get comfortable before resuming talking.

James had been fiddling with an old radio, trying to get it to work on the small solar panel he had rigged up in one of the garage tube lights from outside. When he found a broadcast, he called Gabe in to listen with him.

The broadcast was evidently from somewhere around the Anchorage area. It played the same message, every half hour, then quit after 2 hours.

"Citizens of Alaska, I encourage you to resist all efforts to disarm, disable and dislocate you. There are still numerous groups of our National Guard and State Militia attempting to hold our State together. The massacre staged by the people that are supposed to be "peacekeepers" last fall in Anchorage was documented and is being released to viewers in the Lower 48, even as I speak. The large camp located west of Anchorage has been the scene of desolation and privation all winter. Insufficient clothing and food topping the list of grievances plus many of the barracks have little heating. Fuel ran out to heat the entire facility two months ago. The population has dropped drastically during the winter and there is only a skeleton crew manning the perimeter as the residents are unable to escape and no place to escape to. Please keep them in your prayers, they need all the help they can get. There is no form of government left in Juneau. If anyone manages to make it there and sets up as Governor, please try to do a better job than the last one did. He caught the first flight out of town to Mexico the day we were invaded. There are no plans on any type of food shipments to Alaska any time in the foreseeable future. I will attempt to update my information whenever I can and vow to let you know what I find out as I find it out. May God bless and keep you."

"Well, that is rather depressing, isn't it?" Halya said. "Those poor people in that big camp."

"I think we need to make a cache of supplies and clothing, guns, just a bit of everything, somewhere on up the valley. Just in case we ever have to leave in a hurry." Lynn told them. "I am going to go through my stuff and pack as much as I can spare at present. I think I know where there is an old trapper cabin still standing farther up the valley. It might need some work to make it weather and varmint tight though."

James asked if he could help her and she accepted. They decided to work on the greenhouse as much as possible while she packed in the evenings. Once the greenhouse was planted, they would trek up the valley, looking for the old cabin. Simon would help.

Gabe and Halya said they would do the same on packing extra gear and weapons. Some of the food supplies could go, also, just in case. They would hate to let their supplies fall into enemy hands and nurture them in any way.

They listened for "Alaskan Patriot" but there were no messages that evening from him.

Lynn was up and packing early and had a good start when James and Simon came by to work on the greenhouse. They covered the back wall with junk plywood Gabe had in his junk pile. Then they covered the roof poles in foam board, then some of the plywood, also. It wasn't a beautiful job but it was strong enough for Simon to walk on when he went up to place the white roofing membrane over the whole roof. The ends both had small doors built into them. No one would be getting cornered in the greenhouse.

The water was running clear and a bit more volume now. Lynn put a pole across above the pipe then placed several more to make a walkway over the pipe and keep it from getting damaged by a moose walking on it. Then Lynn fastened a leaning pole from the pipe out a ways to the ground for the water to run down and not make a washout where it dropped and hit the ground directly under it without making any noise.

Simon came back, carrying the clear greenhouse panels and they were installed across the south facing wall. The inside back and side walls were covered in the white foam board. It would insulate and reflect light inside.

They placed some large logs along each side of a walkway down the center of the building, from door to door. Then they placed plastic up the logs for the dirt beds and the bottom logs used as the base under the back wall and the clear wall. The topsoil in buckets was brought in and dumped in the makeshift planting beds. Lynn wanted to bring over the chickens and let them fertilize the greenhouse until they could start planting, but was afraid something would happen to them. She would bring the coop cleanings and put them under the rows deep enough not to burn new roots but fertilize the plants as they grew.

They walked over to her house, and she prepared some lunch while they loaded backpacks to take some supplies with them. She fed and changed Aurora and placed her in her chest pouch, then hefted up her backpack and rifle.

Lynn had not been to the old cabin in a couple of years and never from this direction. She almost missed it and the men didn't see it until they were almost at the door.

The cabin had been built right into a thicket of spruce trees and blended in so well it looked like it grew there. Lynn knocked on the door and waited a bit, then found the hidden key behind the fake log piece by a window shutter. She unlocked the padlock that was hidden under another log that was hollowed out and covered the doorknob. Another swung back with the door as she opened it, covering the hinges. James was looking at all these things with great interest.

The inside of the cabin was a surprise to the men. It was a large room downstairs, divided into three spaces and a ladder stairs up to several rooms for sleeping or storage. Lynn opened a couple of the shutters so they could see what they were doing and took her load up the ladder to the last room upstairs. She figured she would start filling the rooms from the back to the front. There were already several rifles and plenty of ammunition stored in the old cabin. She was glad to see no sign of leaking or rodent damage.

She emptied her pack and then the men's packs as they brought them up for her. This cabin was a marvelous place to stay or live in. They asked about the owner and she told them he had been killed in a freak car accident a few years ago near Fairbanks. A car came over the embankment and hit him right in the driver's side front and door, killing him instantly. Very few people knew where this cabin was located. She felt fairly confident no one would claim it now.

By the time they returned home, they were all dragging. James even carried Aurora the last couple of miles. Lynn felt like she was walking on cooked spaghetti legs she was so tired.

James and Simon left her at her door and she went in, cared for Aurora and was asleep before she knew what happened. Halya brought her dinner over and she slept right through it. So she covered her up on the couch, added some wood to the fire, locked the door and went home.

Chapter 17

Lynn awoke several hours later, famished. She found the plate of food and ate it cold. It still tasted delicious. She changed and fed the baby and went right back to sleep. When she finally woke up it was a bit later than usual for her, but she felt a lot better.

She hadn't made her rice the night before, so opened a jar of something, heated it on the wood stove and mashed some for Aurora, mixed some up with the dwindling supply of cat food and shared. As she came out her door, James was just about to knock.

"Oops, how are you doing this morning? We missed you at dinner," he said.

"Oh, I feel great. Nothing like 12 hours of sleep to perk a person right up," she replied.

They got right on packing more supplies up to the cabin. Gabe and Halya each packed a load, then Halya volunteered to babysit and fix dinner while the rest of them continued packing. Their next trip back, she had lunch ready for them and they ate, then left immediately again. By the time they were ready to quit for the night, they had the old cabin very well stocked and they felt proud of getting so much accomplished in such a short time. Halya continued to pack more supplies and clothing, bedding and miscellaneous odds and ends she thought they should have if they ever needed to move out in a hurry.

During the night, they heard the sound of many planes flying overhead and figured this summer's invasion had begun. Shortly after, they saw huge billowing glowing clouds from the direction of Fairbanks. They didn't know whether or not the planes were bombing the town or if they were meeting some very heavy resistance to landing.

Lynn, Simon and James planted the greenhouse the next morning, very early. Lynn hooked up her soaker hose watering system to the rainwater tank hanging on the back of the greenhouse. She used water from buckets left warming in the greenhouse to water the seedlings. The water directly out of the pipe may have been considered a warm spring, but it was still very cold water.

Lynn had been planting a few seeds here and there whenever she walked through the woods and even had planted some along the small river on the way to the old cabin. She thought a regular garden would show up too much from a distance or the air and would be investigated. But a few plants here and there should be okay. She would wait on the very delicate seeds and the potatoes. They didn't have enough to chance losing to a late frost. She did put a few potatoes in an above ground planter system using old logs and building it higher as the plants grew, right beside the greenhouse. The potatoes were sprouting and getting very wrinkled, so they were trying to keep all of them now to plant.

Onion roots and garlic cloves that they had started in the house were planted here and there around the houses. The cabbage hearts they had rooted were also all planted near the houses to be kept track of.

That night, there were broadcasts from both of the ones they had heard from before. The one near Anchorage had more information, but the "Alaskan Patriot" had closer to home news for them.

Planes had attempted to land at each location, to be met by small rocket fire. The planes were not expecting resistance and had no escorts, they were transporters. They had sustained heavy losses at both locations. There had been an interim government of sorts set up near Anchorage and they were flat telling Washington D.C. to back off and call off their pet "peacekeepers".

The radio was now broadcasting on extremely high power which was considered illegal, but since government was making the entire State an illegal entity, why not? They also had managed to hack into a satellite and were broadcasting to the world, with video of everything that Alaska was going through. That was shut down almost immediately, but still got the word out to enough people that it was now being talked about all over the world.

"Alaskan Patriot" let them know that not a single plane managed to land or unload troops in Fairbanks and the runways at the nearby Bases were too damaged to land on, either. It was hinted that the interceptor missiles near Delta were now in Alaskan hands and ready to be used if needed. Both broadcasts hinted at possible relief being offered by an undisclosed source.

"I don't know if the offered help would end up being worse than what is already here," Gabe said.

"Too bad no one said just who is doing the offering," James added.

"All we can do is pray whoever it is, actually helps and doesn't set us up to invite in worse conditions that what is already being foisted on us," Lynn said.

"I hope whomever is setting themselves up as our governing body near Anchorage has enough sense not to just jump at the first offer and ignore the ramifications of the future with them as either allies or overlords, whichever it ends up being." Simon put in.

Everyone went their separate ways for the evening but most had a hard time sleeping. There was just too much information still unknown.

As the trees started leafing out and flowers bloomed all around on the hill, everyone started carrying some garden seeds with them to plant when and wherever they found some open ground where it wouldn't be too noticeable but still open enough to grow a crop. Barley and oats were raked into the ground wherever there was native grass stalks from last summer. Potatoes were planted everywhere.

The greenhouse was working out beautifully. The plants growing on the soil over the warm spring were almost leaping up. The squash plants were setting blossoms already. If they were allowed to produce, there would be plenty of assorted squashes for the coming year. The tomatoes and cucumbers were starting to bloom, also. On the three sides of the greenhouse that didn't have greenhouse panels, they leaned old dead spruce saplings and brush to confuse the outline from a distance. Maybe no one would notice it if they were walking through the woods.

James and Simon returned one evening so proud of themselves they practically glowed. They had reset the explosives on all the houses. Now anyone just walking in the doors would be fine, but if the ones setting the explosives attempted to disarm them to enter, they would blow themselves up. They didn't know if the original bomb placers followed any sort of plan so that anyone in the same organization would know where and how they were placed and how to disarm, but thought they must.

Of course the original group didn't place a very high value on human life, even one of their own. At least innocent people wouldn't get blown up by accident, now.

There were no more planes flying, for several days. Then another flight went over and circled over Fairbanks but did not land. Parachutes filled the sky and were met by deadly fire from the ground. There may not be the same population in Fairbanks as before, but it seemed that all of them were armed and willing to defend their homes.

The radio message that night confirmed their conjectures and added that Anchorage was doing the same. There had been a mass attack on the large camp west of Anchorage and the guards were overrun from the inside as well as the outside of camp, once the inmates knew what was happening. The results for the guards were not pretty. Now the remaining inmates were armed as best as they could manage from the stores in the camp and they joined up with the Militia and National Guard that were still resisting. Many of the former military from the Bases had also joined the Militia and brought weapons and knowledge with them. This summer would not be an easy takeover by the "Peacekeepers" in any way. Now the residents knew what to expect and were willing to retaliate in kind.

Lynn was feeling better about their chances of surviving now. Maybe enough of the news reaching the outside world would convince people of the truth of what was happening here. Maybe world opinion would sway the people in control. Yes, and maybe monkeys would fly.

They had been working very hard for several days and had James and Simon's house enclosed and covered. It was small but they would be comfortable in it. Another pipe with wire through it to a bell linked it to Gabe and Halya's home. It wasn't much, but it would alert them if there was an emergency.

They were all working on cutting the downed trees from winter into smaller pieces with the bow saws and dragging or carrying pieces home towards having wood for the coming winter. That was always the major thought in the back of everyone's mind. Will we have enough wood for the winter? No one enjoys being cold and the thought of freezing to death was not high on anyone's list of things they really wanted to do, ever.

One of Lynn's cats woke her up during the night. As she tried to place a sound she heard, she realized there were people in her home and she immediately felt curls of fear lacing up through her, choking her. She reached down beside the bed and her fingers closed over the handle of the weed burner from her greenhouse. She slowly pulled it up so when she swung her legs over the side of the bed and stood, it was in her hands. Her fingers found the control knob as the person in front of her fumbled trying to light a match to find a lamp or candle.

He did not realize she was awake or standing in front of him and when the match flared, the leaking propane from the weed burner swooshed into his face, setting him on fire.

A startled exclamation on her left swung Lynn around toward another man stepping toward her. The torch was going well now and she torched the man who chose to rush at her instead of retreat. The third man was stepping toward the bed Aurora was in and Lynn didn't hesitate. She torched him from behind. No one was going to grab her baby.

She grabbed Aurora and headed for the door. When she opened it, the fresh air increased the flames and the screams from inside were horrific. She still had the lit torch in her other hand and didn't hesitate to flare the man rushing toward her as she came out the door. He screamed and fell, clawing at his face.

James and Simon came running from the garage and she waved them into the house. She pulled the room darkening curtains back so light flooded the room. The smell was horrible but the sight of the burnt men had her rushing outside to lose whatever last night's dinner had been. Simon joined her. When they finished retching, they went back to try helping James. James and Simon each grabbed a man by his feet and dragged them outside. Then came back for the other one. The men wore uniforms and they found the blue helmets in various locations around the room and outside.

Lynn stayed outside near her house while James and Simon went to check on Gabe and Halya. They were fine and surprised everyone was up and about. It was still very early in the morning. Then they were staggered by Lynn having just dispatched 4 of the enemy.

"Why does everyone come from that direction? We thought it would be the safest place out here." Halya exclaimed.

"I think we need to look around through the woods and see if they have a camp anywhere around here," James said. "They have probably been watching us and thought she would be the weak link."

"Gee, thanks," Lynn told him.

"Well it is obvious you aren't, but how were they to know? The poor innocents, they found the tiger," James teased her.

Chapter 18

They hurried up and dragged the bodies over to the edge of the woods. They ate some breakfast although Simon and Lynn still weren't too hungry. Then Halya offered to babysit while the rest went hunting for a camp in the area. She would start cleanup on Lynn's house. Halya said she would be willing to go, but she was not very good in the woods at being quiet.

The ground was still slightly damp from a rain shower, so they would make less noise than usual, walking through the woods.

They found the small camp just a little ways up the hill beyond Lynn's home. From the amount of packs and supplies, only the four dead men had camped here. They must have seen her enter her house as it was hard to find. Maybe they were unaware there were even others living near her. The camp didn't have a look of long usage, so maybe last night was their first in the area. It wasn't as though they could ask one of them.

They picked up all the gear and carried everything back to Lynn's. Halya was coming out the door with a bundle of laundry.

"I thought you would rather do laundry in the greenhouse and hang it in there to dry. I changed the bedding and mopped the floor. That's about all that can be managed besides leaving this door open. I also lit a couple of scented candles and put some mint in a pot of water on the stove," Halya told Lynn.

Both babies were asleep in the baby bed. The house smelled of mint and the cinnamon candles.

"Wow, you are amazing. I figured I was going to have to either build a new house or live with that odor," Lynn told her.

Halya held up a spray bottle and told her to let some of the mint water cool down a bit and spray the entire house with it. That should remove any lingering odor. Little Joseph woke up, so Halya picked him up and told Lynn to come over when Aurora woke up for some lunch.

The chickens were taken outside every day in their little chicken tractor. The wheels on the front made it easy to move around. Being long and narrow, it fit through the small side door. The small chicks from the first broody hen were growing fast on their diet of bugs and weeds.

The mint planted around all the cabin fronts helped keep bugs out of the houses. The second family of baby chicks were still confined to the garage as they were small enough to escape through the wire mesh on the little tractor. Simon found some bags of chicken feed in a couple of the sheds near where he found the chickens and brought it home. It was doled out to the mother hens and chicks. The rest were doing well on foraging.

They would always look raggedy with their missing combs and wattles, but they were all gaining weight and looking much better. Now, eggs were being used for meals and everyone was enjoying them very much. They figured if they saw Jesse again, they would share a pair of chickens so they could grow their own flock.

Lynn had lunch with Halya, the men had taken something to eat with them when they hauled the bodies away. They didn't want them ever found anywhere near their homes. They loaded them on the akio and were dragging them down the valley toward the burned out truck from last year.

After lunch, Lynn took Aurora and her bag of laundry to the greenhouse. She wanted all sign erased, today, including odor. She had a heavy duty clamp fastened to a tree that she clamped one end of large items to, to wring them out. After clamping one end, she twisted from the other and got them as dry as possible. Blankets, sheets and work jeans, mostly or sometimes a small throw rug.

Then she hung them in the greenhouse. She would have preferred hanging the clothes outside for the breeze to fluff and dry, but the sight of clothing hanging outdoors would certainly give away their location.

The plants in the greenhouse were starting to crowd her clothes drying space. Soon she might have to go back to hanging them around in her small house or ask Gabe about putting lines up in his shop. It was used for so much more than a shop now that she doubted he ever got much time to enjoy in there.

The greenhouse was handier as laundry was done in water from the pipe. But she guessed during the summer the river water would be fine for washing clothes. As far as she knew, there had been no more spraying.

Simon was on one of his foraging runs when he heard vehicles coming on the road. He ducked down behind some trees in the bar ditch and waited. Soon some pickups and a couple of military looking vehicles came into view.

They stopped on the main road, near the store and several people got out. They stood around looking at the buildings and discussing something. One of the pickups blared a few bars of "Dixie". Somehow, this motley crew did not fit the image of the invaders. Simon was debating with himself about the possibility of showing himself and finding out just who these people were and what they wanted, when he saw his Dad walk out onto the road from the other side.

James kept his weapon down at his side and hoped he wasn't making the biggest mistake of his life. He walked slowly towards the silent men grouped around the vehicles. He raised his other hand in greeting and stopped.

One of the men in the other group walked toward him and held out his hand to shake. James wasn't sure whether or not that was to pull him off balance or not so stepped back. The other man dropped his hand but smiled. He was a fairly tall lanky older man with a pleasant face and slightly curling hair, neatly trimmed and combed.

"Well, you have no reason to trust me, so I can see your point. I'm Wayne Porter, I used to live up on Skyridge Drive near Fairbanks. Me and the rest of this group are trying to find out how many of us are left and to hand out some extra supplies we sort of inherited. If you want a couple of small rocket launchers and the rockets to go with them, we have plenty. We are also hoping to find folks willing to plant gardens and raise some animals towards feeding the folks still alive around town. We have some started plants that we are planting along the roadways as we travel."

James thanked him for the offer and asked if it wasn't a bit late to try planting now? Seeds wouldn't have a chance of maturing.

"Well, I can give you some packets towards next year, then. I've never done any gardening and am trying to learn as we go. We are going to see about driving out to Manley if the road is okay. They have the Hot Springs and maybe we can help if they need any. We brought materials to help them on Greenhouses, if they need it." Wayne told him. "We've been helping, up at the Chena Hot Springs. Their buildings needed some new glass installed after the gentle 'peacekeepers' got through, last summer."

"Good wishes on your project and make sure they know who you are as soon as you start into town over there. If there are any people still there, they won't be in a good mood." James told him.

"Yeah, we been noticing that. Your friend on the other side of the road has had his sights on me the whole time I've been talking to you." Wayne said.

James told him there were still blue helmets wandering around out through the woods here, to be careful, they may have parachuted in somewhere farther north and now working their way south in small groups.

Wayne looked genuinely surprised. "What? When have you seen any? Really? There are more left out here? We were told before we left town that this entire road system was free and clear, that we didn't have to worry on this trip like we have on some of the others."

James assured him there indeed were more invaders wandering around and to pay attention if they wanted to make the return trip in one piece.

Wayne walked back to his group and told them what James had told him. They immediately straightened up and looked around better. When he pointed out Simon sitting beside the road with his rifle at the ready, a couple of them seemed upset. He told them to cool it, the kid could have taken them out at any time if he had a mind to, and they should thank him for showing them how easily this could become a one way trip for them.

He turned and waved to James and Simon. Then he reached into the front seat of one of the trucks and removed a box and sat it beside the road. Everyone got back in the vehicles and soon they were on their way north again.

After they were out of sight, James approached the box hesitantly, reaching out with a stick to move a top flap to the side to see inside the box better. A couple of green plants were visible and some plastic bags with small paper packets in them. It was a strange bomb if it were a bomb, so he picked up the box, motioned to Simon and they headed down the hill.

Lynn was happy to see the plants and the seeds. She said the plants were herbs and would improve their meals in the future.

She planted the dill by her cabin near the mint and took the basil down to Halya's doorway. There were a few oregano plants also and she placed them closer to the house, hoping the heat from the house would be enough to winter them over if they covered them.

She worked some fertilizer in around the plants to help them recover from transplant shock. With the onions and garlic they were growing, they would still have some flavor in their meals. She placed the packets of seeds in the bag she had hers in, saving for next season. These were kept in the coolest part of her house.

In the bottom of the box, she found a couple of pieces of horseradish root and a piece of ginger root. The horseradish, she planted near her chimney by the rock ledge. The dirt was rich and she worked more fertilizer in as she planted there, also. The ginger she wasn't too sure of and planted in a 5 gallon bucket of rich soil.

During dinner, they all discussed the group of men heading out the road. They hoped they truly were what they seemed. The plants and seeds seemed to say they were. James had not given his name nor the names of anyone else here. That group didn't know if there were an entire community or just the two people they had seen.

They would remain cautious and if they met the group again, they would not bring them down here to their homes. It was better to error on the side of caution than to welcome them with open arms and end up dead.

The radio reports continued. Sometimes it seemed like the invaders were backing off, then they would do something to bring Alaska under their control. They no longer held any prisoners in Alaska and there were reports of small groups of them moving south from some place they had either landed, parachuted into or wintered over farther north. Lynn didn't believe any had survived the winter in Alaska. They seemed very ill prepared and unwilling to adapt.

James, Simon, Gabe and Halya agreed. They still did not seem to change their operations to suit the climate and conditions. This worked in favor of Alaska. Everyone at the table hoped leadership continued thinking like that.

Over the next several days, they saw sign of small groups of people moving through the area so stayed very close to home. In the evenings, they carefully searched for any sign of camps. The men found one group of four camped near Lynn's house up the hill. They used their small arms, 22LR handguns and took care of that portion of the problem. Their main problem would be how to get rid of the evidence. For these four, they dumped them in the outhouse. The weapons, clothes and packs went home with Gabe, James and Simon.

Chapter 19

Halya and Lynn covered their rough floors with quilts and blankets as the babies were crawling now. The floors were rough enough to cause splinters so everyone had to take off shoes or boots at the door before coming in. So when they heard footsteps coming toward the door but not stopping to take off boots, Lynn stepped behind the door and Halya grabbed the babies and headed into her bedroom with them.

The door swung open and the person stepped into the room. Lynn swung and at the last minute recognized the person she was about to give a king sized headache.

"Jesse!"

She deflected the blow for the most part and he ducked with great reflexes to only receive a glancing blow on his shoulder. The shovel clattered to the floor as Lynn rushed up to make sure he would be okay.

"Okay, I earned that one," he said. He rubbed his shoulder a bit but said he really wasn't broken and was glad she recognized him when she was swinging, not after she laid him out on the floor.

Halya came back out of the bedroom and set the babies back down on the floor. Jesse noticed the quilts and quickly removed his shoes.

Lynn told him that is how she knew he wasn't someone that lived there. He told her he wondered if she lived right behind the door coshing anyone that came through it.

The men returned while they were standing there and he waited until they were all indoors before he told them why he was there.

"I hiked in to Manley Hot Springs a while back to see if anyone made it, there. We knew several people that lived there. Very few of the people we knew survived the past year. While I was there, a group of fellows from Fairbanks came out. They brought a lot of supplies and set up helping repair the greenhouses and planting a lot of plants they brought with them. Most folks were a little jaundiced in their outlook, but the people just kept on working. I think they are on the up and up. I'm really hoping I am right about that. I'm thinking of moving Marilee and little James down there and working in the growing food business. There are not enough people left there to grow food on the scale possible and everyone is going to be needing food soon."

While he took a drink of water, James asked, "Did they treat everyone okay and no off remarks or hints of anything not quite right?"

"Not that I noticed. I was really trying to catch them off guard, too. They must have thought I have the attention span of a gnat since I jumped from subject to subject so often. But no matter what random subject I talked about, they had the right answers."

"Simon and I only saw them for a little while. I wasn't sure what to think and only spoke to one person. The rest stayed by the vehicles and Simon stayed over at the edge of the road with a good view and range on the whole lot," James told him.

"We figured if they stopped by on their way back, that we wouldn't bring them down here, but be polite and helpful in any other way. It might be nice to have some friends in town," James continued.

"I was going to try making it to town, but I am running low on supplies, could I spend the day here, and take a lunch when I leave later this evening? I didn't want to camp out any more than I have to and it has taken me almost 3 days to get here from Manley." Jesse told them.

"If you guys can dismantle the bomb on my pickup and put the battery back in it, you can take it to town," Lynn offered.

James and Simon thought they could manage that and she took them over to get the battery, 5 gallons of gas and the keys to see if they could get it running without blowing themselves up. The men were back in a couple of hours.

"Piece of cake. Whoever set the bomb was not experienced at it. We brought the whole thing back with us in case we ever want to booby-trap anything."

"We even checked over the rest of the pickup to make sure that was the only bomb on it. If you don't mind, Jesse, we would like to ride in with you and then we would never have to leave the pickup unattended." James said.

"Since we ain't walking, let's go right now. I really want to see what I can find in town for the greenhouses and for some possible books on northern growing." Jesse spoke up.

The others agreed and they grabbed a couple of sandwiches Halya made while they spoke and headed out the door.

Gabe, Halya and Lynn did busy work around the main house the entire time the men were gone. As they walked into the yard, several hours later, Lynn asked Halya what would they have done if somehow the men never came back? Just paced around until they dropped?

Halya was giggling when the men reached the house. She excused herself to go check on the pot of soup on the stove and the rest dropped their heavy packs and sat leaning against the outside wall of the house. They started to open the packs outside but Gabe suggested they go in the garage because they really didn't want to have one of the small groups of marauders catch them outside admiring whatever was in the packs. The others looked a bit sheepish then Simon exclaimed, "You should see what is still up in the back of the pickup."

They had traded furs and placer gold for tools, ammunition, some grenades and socks.

"Some guy was set up, trading, from supplies he salvaged from one of the military bases. He had all sorts of underwear and socks, which is mostly what we took, along with some cargo type pants. Then he offered us a cow about to calve if we would haul one load of supplies for him to his place in the hills this side of Fairbanks. We weren't too sure, with it being Lynn's pickup, how we should handle that. Then he showed us what he needed hauled and we probably would have carried it if we had to, for him. His wife is crippled from a beating she received from a 'peacekeeper' for being dressed improperly in public. Somehow the man acquired a wheelchair that is battery operated but has a solar panel charger for it. We loaded up that chair and the charger unit and he closed up shop for the day. We got to their house and unloaded everything. His wife hobbled out using crutches to thank us and she was crying." Simon ran out of words, choked up in remembrance.

James took up the story, "The fellow helped us knock together a rack for the truck and we loaded the cow and some bales of hay around her to cushion her ride out. We have to get back to the truck and figure out how to unload her without hurting her."

The pickup was parked at the end of a seldom used old road that came farther down the hill from behind the store than Lynn's driveway did and was probably better hidden under the trees than if they had parked in Lynn's yard.

The men carried some heavy planks back up the hill and they made a ramp from the back of the truck to the bank they backed the truck against. They tied a coat over the placid cow's head so she couldn't see exactly what they were walking her over and she unloaded as though it happened every day.

The cow was walked down the hill to the homes and found a place near the chicken coop in the garage. The bales of hay were unloaded and the cheese making supplies the man's wife had added to the load. Then they fueled up the pickup, Gabe and Halya gave Jesse a ride home, as far as the Hutlinana, known as the Hoot by most of the locals. His backpack was heavily loaded with the books he had traded for. There were some pamphlets from the Ag school at the University in Fairbanks. He even managed to get a couple of books on home medical diagnostics and treatment. His load was padded with socks and underwear. Tucked in corners were some small clothing items Lynn had made for little James.

After they left, James asked Lynn why she had them take Jesse home.

"I don't think Halya has been away from the house at all since quite a while before this started and it is good for her to get out once in a while," Lynn answered.

"I think we need to build another large shelter here, either for animals or equipment, but Gabe's backhoe is definitely getting crowded in the garage," Simon put in.

"We will need to build to store hay we are going to have to cut for winter, anyway, so we should ask Gabe which he wants to build for and get started when he gets back." James told him.

It was almost three hours later before Gabe and Halya returned. They took the time up on Ptarmigan Pass to pick the half ripe blueberries that were so thick up there. Even carrying Joseph in his pouch didn't slow down the picking and they would be drying and canning the next few days. The two buckets were almost full, that Gabe hauled out of the backseat and carried down the hill. Simon went back up and took the battery back out of the pickup. No use leaving it in case someone else decided they needed it. The pickup was parked right back in its tracks where it spent the winter.

Over dinner, they discussed the need for hay and storage for it. Also the chickens would need grain of some sort. As the wild grasses started to head, they needed to clip the heads and dry them for the chickens and where the grass was thick enough, cut it for hay. This would be an obvious sign there were people in the area. Unfortunately, most of the cleared ground with grass and clover growing was along the highway right of way. Gabe had a weed wacker and so did Lynn, but they were gas motors and not very quiet. They may just have to take their chances.

Chapter 20

They listened for news, hoping to hear there would be no more intruders. Instead, they heard that fighting had increased around the Anchorage area and the small groups coming down from the north toward Fairbanks were confirmed parachute drops, although no new ones had been sighted.

So, take their chances and cut hay or remain hidden and starve the cow? They decided to cut hay. They would try to always be two people teams, one to cut, one to watch for intruders. Some days, they would work as three person teams, one cutting, one gathering and one watching. Gabe moved his backhoe out of the garage and put it under the trees with more sticks and brush fastened over it to confuse the outline.

Now that James and Simon were living in their own little house, the shop no longer housed people, so they moved all the work benches to one side and made the rest into a stall and hay storage with one corner dedicated to a chicken coop. The cow was a very small cow, one bred purposely to be a small farm dairy cow. She wasn't much larger than a large goat. She was possibly a small jersey designed for very small farms. Lynn had never seen a full grown cow as small, maybe 600 pounds. She was adorable with her pale tan body, dark accents and enormous eyes. Her eyelashes could give any woman a complex, long, curled and thick. She calved with no trouble a few days later. A bull calf. Lynn renewed her milking skills.

Lynn snapped a lead rope on her halter and took her over to a patch of grass near the river, daily. The cow started grazing as though she had never been hauled in the back of a pickup, wedged in with bales of hay and a bag of feed. They would save the hay for days they couldn't graze her or winter. Lynn was happy to see she browsed some on the birch and willow brush, also. They could always cut small brush for her, for feed, also.

The next time they listened to the radio, they heard good news, they hoped. At least it was good news for them. Either the invaders were a little sketchy on geography or just didn't care, but they had attacked a small town in Canada near the Alaska Border. Word immediately hit Toronto and Canada was not amused.

The spray drifting into Canada last year was bad enough, but this time Canadian citizens had been taken from their homes and incarcerated for a while. People were hearing rumors and starting to ask questions. Canada was sending some people to see for themselves and asked the Alaskans not to assume they would be on the "other" side if they came. Their planes would be well marked.

The President was blustering and making excuses already, so it seemed he was already looking for scapegoats in his administration to blame this on. He would have a hard time blaming Bush for this one.

Then the UN Secretary announced he was retiring. This caused worldwide ripples. As soon as he announced, the President jumped on him as the handiest one to blame for the entire fiasco. The man took exception to that and pulled out everything showing the President had approached him about a problem with a rogue State.

Washington DC was in an uproar and no one was sure who they could trust. It's not like they could trust anyone before, but now it was extremely dangerous. The balance of power was shifting and no one had a clear view of where it would settle. No one knew who they needed to kiss up to, to assure they didn't lose their little piece of the pie.

Someone on the other side of the world figured it was too good a chance to pass up and launched a missile at Alaska, but the people manning the anti-missile site near Delta did their job perfectly and took it out even as the planes from Canada were approaching Fairbanks and Anchorage to see just what was really happening.

Then the radio started breaking up and the signal was lost. As a cliffhanger, it worked. No one got any sleep that night.

James and Simon were on the hill across the river from their house when they heard sounds of movement through the trees behind them. James stayed in place and Simon beat all records for getting back to the houses to alert everyone else. Gabe and Halya were sitting in their living room, talking and only had to grab weapons. Gabe got a small rocket launcher from the first encounter with the invaders from the closet by the door. Halya loaded Simon up with the rockets for it. They headed across the river to meet up with James and Halya went on up river to Lynn's.

The babies were the only ones still sleeping, so they took the chance rather than have a baby make a noise and alert the enemy of their locations. Far better to leave the babies in safe places. Lynn and Halya both loaded up with weapons and a small grenade launcher they had salvaged from the ambush up the road during the winter. They moved over across the river and came in behind where Simon said the noise was coming from.

They had just about reached the small meadow when they heard sounds of a lot of people milling about, setting up camp. It sounded like a fairly large group. They worked their way down hill until they met up with James, Simon and Gabe. They would check and see just which side they were meeting up with, out here. Would these be invaders or some of the State's own National Guard or Militia?

Simon slipped away and inched his way to a vantage point overlooking the group setting up camp. When he returned, he said they were wearing the ever present blue helmets of the UN group and there were a lot of them. They all moved to the observation point Simon had used and looked the encampment over thoroughly. Then Lynn tugged on Gabe's sleeve and pointed to a separate group over in the edge of the trees.

It appeared they had a fairly large group of prisoners that looked a lot worse for wear. Every time a guard walked by them, he kicked or hit one of them.

James and Simon offered to go around and see about arming some of the prisoners and see if they could help out if a diversion happened on this side of the meadow. The grenade launcher would probably be better to use at this range than the rockets as they were not positive on how much damage the rocket would do and they didn't want to take out the prisoners, also.

Gabe explained the grenade launcher to Halya and set her up to start launching in 10 minutes. That would give them all time to encircle the camp and arm the prisoners if possible.

Lynn would circle back and make sure no one snuck up on Halya while she was working. They had spotted the camp guards and would work their way around camp, taking out the guards as they went. Each one had some of the grenades, also. Maybe no one could pinpoint where the launcher was set up until it was too late.

James and Simon made it around their side of camp the fastest as they had to reach the prisoners and see about arming some of them. They acquired the weapons from the guards they immobilized on their way to add to the ones they were carrying. By the time they reached the prisoners, they fairly bristled with weapons and since the guards there were all watching the prisoners, they were the simplest of all to disable. They warned the prisoners as they handed them weapons and all faded back into the trees about the other ones helping set up the attack and not to shoot until they were positive. No one mentioned they were women.

Ten minutes on the dot, Halya lobbed the first grenade into the center of camp and immediate chaos ensued. She kept launching, Lynn kept throwing and the men around the camp started shooting and throwing the occasional grenade themselves. Later, James said it was like shooting fish in a barrel.

There might have been prisoners taken, except the newly released prisoners didn't bother to even try.

They had not received pleasant treatment and each one wanted some revenge.

As the noise quieted down and only a gurgle here and there as the former prisoners made their way through camp broke the stillness of the night. Everyone edged out into the opening and checked to make double sure no one was going to suddenly rise up and open fire on them. Lynn and Halya walked into camp as Gabe and James stood in the center. Simon walked right behind the women and carried the launchers. Someone said, "Women, we've been saved by women."

"I think the men had a lot to do with that," Lynn said.

"Oh, I know, but I never thought I would see the day that I would be rescued by ladies and I thank you very much. I doubt if we could have done as well without those grenades steadily coming in." the same voice said.

James had set up a makeshift clinic and was doctoring wounds. Some were pretty bad and would require better care than he could handle out here in the middle of the woods. Two were quite serious and needed immediate care, so Lynn asked Simon if he wanted to put the battery in her pickup again.

Gabe was going through the papers carried by the head man for the invaders and found some very interesting information that he thought should be taken in if they were going to haul the most wounded to town.

Simon pulled down to the meadow in Lynn's pickup. He mentioned the trailer still parked near the buildings up the hill and they went back for it. All the bodies and wounded were loaded into the trailer and pickup. The bed of the pickup was covered in sleeping bags to make a large pallet of sorts and the wounded were situated on it as well as possible with some inside the pickup also.

No one wanted to drive in. James and Simon already had gone, Lynn didn't want to leave Aurora. Gabe and Halya didn't want to go either. Lynn, being the only one that had not been away from the place in a long time was chosen to go. Halya and Simon went back to the house to get Aurora and Simon brought her back up the hill with the bag Halya packed for her. After all, it was her pickup that kept getting used by everyone.

Lynn strapped Aurora into a container she used in the pickup, right beside her driver's seat. Aurora watched everyone with her huge green eyes and never made a sound.

"Uh, ma'am? How old is your baby?" the soft voice from the back seat startled Lynn. She wasn't used to anyone asking her questions about her daughter.

"She was born in early April. Not sure exactly what day," she replied.

"You had her out here?" the same soft voice asked.

"Yes, no place else was handy at the time," she answered.

"Wow, so you not only rescue idiots that get taken prisoner and know how to shoot a gun, but you had a baby out here," he sounded surprised.

Lynn was concentrating on driving slowly and not lose any passengers in the pickup or bodies off the trailer so didn't say anything.

"Ma'am? I didn't mean to upset you, I'm just amazed is all. It's not every day I get to meet a real hero type woman. You do know if you had not saved us tonight, none of us would have lived beyond tomorrow? They made it quite plain they intended on executing every one of us. They were going to make a game out of it, tonight after they had their dinner."

"How did they catch so many of you? I have been wondering," she asked.

"We've been working with the Militia and had a radio set up, sending out news and gathering information. We've managed to contact people in Canada and the Lower 48 that actually believe us. We were broadcasting when they caught us."

"I think we were listening, then. We thought maybe the power went off or something. We certainly have enjoyed listening to the news all winter and thank you all for doing that. You gave us hope," she told him.

"Taylor, the guy on the pallet in the back was the announcer. I sure hope we find someone that can patch him up. He is a good man to have on our side," the young man coughed and was silent a while.

Lynn was very close to town now and did not have any idea where to go, now that she was here. She pulled in to the Quick Care building as soon as she got into town and circled the trailer around to be ready to leave if it were not a good spot to be. A couple of the walking wounded jumped out of the back of the pickup and headed for the doors. Soon people were edging out into sight from various locations.

Someone recognized the pickup. "Hey, where is Jesse? He was driving this truck a while back."

"I loaned it to him and the two men that rode in with him," she told them.

"Yeah, they did say a girl let them use her truck. We thought that was a story," someone else said.

More people were coming out of the clinic pushing gurneys and wheelchairs. The men in the bed of the truck were unloaded first, then the ones in her backseat. People rushed to assist the ones having trouble walking. She waited until all the injured were inside. Then she didn't know what to do about the load in the trailer. She certainly wasn't taking them back home with her.

About that time, a vehicle pulled in next to her. The man getting out to come over was a person that commanded respect before he even opened his mouth. He looked very tired.

"I see you have some trash for me to go through," he said to her.

"Yes Sir. The sooner I get them off my hands the sooner I can go home, Sir," she answered.

"Would you mind dragging their sorry carcasses along a bit farther and we can get them out of this parking lot?" he asked.

"Yes Sir. I can do that, Sir," she replied.

"You're a civilian now, you don't have to Sir me."

"I know, Sir, but I respect the job you are doing and it hasn't been that long since I was used to this, Sir," she told him.

He quirked an eyebrow at her and she said, "Afghanistan, Sir. I've been out just over two years."

"Nasty business over there. Glad you made it home in one piece. Carry on, Soldier." He walked back to his vehicle and his driver motioned her to follow.

Chapter 21

Later, when she was back home, she described to the rest how the day had gone. She had followed them out to the military Base that was being used by the National Guard, the Militia and as many of the original soldiers as stood by their oaths to defend the Constitution. There were several hundred out there now.

While they were unloading her trailer, a large plane with the maple leaf of Canada had circled twice, then when no opposition was encountered, landed on the repaired runway. They immediately started unloading cases of food.

She had stood there, open mouthed and listened as the Commander catalogued the grievances against Alaska by the President and the UN "Peacekeepers". The representatives from Canada thanked him, loaded the bodies into the plane and took off back for Canada.

Maybe, just maybe, something good would come of all of this for Alaska.

Later, they heard that a similar experience played out in Anchorage, without the load of dead bodies.

However, there just happened to be video shot from a different angle of the assassination of the Congressional members last year that clearly showed the UN "Peacekeepers" firing on the plane and the fact finding mission. It even showed the other photographer setting up to be out of their line of fire before the plane landed. Then he and the reporter being escorted back into a building.

The delegation was shown the camp west of Anchorage where so many had lost their lives and the mass graves around Anchorage where a good portion of the former population now resided. No one had a good word for any aspect of the invasion. There had been no warning, no negotiations and no chance to even know why they were being invaded. It was an Act of War against one of the States making up the United States. If it could happen to one, it could happen to any of them.

James took the cow out browsing while Lynn started making some cheese from the excess milk they had. The calf was fed half the milk at each milking as the small cow gave just over a gallon at each milking. If they had grain to feed her, she might have increased production, but they were happy getting about a gallon and a half per day, total.

While leading the cow back to the shop, he heard the sound of movement up the hill. Listening carefully, it sounded like a lot of people quietly moving south. He put the cow up with extra hay and water and notified everyone else. They always kept the most needed items packed in backpacks near the doors, just in case and this sounded on a scale to validate that readiness.

Simon breathlessly came in the door as they were picking up last minute items to carry along with them.

"Peacekeepers, an entire pack of them, marching down the road toward Fairbanks. I think we need to get up to the cabin as soon as possible."

"We are almost ready to leave, Son. Get your pack and help Lynn with the baby stuff, if you would, please?" James asked.

They crossed the low little river and worked their way north, staying in the trees as much as possible. When they reached the cabin, they would have missed it is Lynn hadn't of turned and walked over to it. They were careful going through the tall grass and brush so not much was knocked down to mark their passage.

Lynn went around the outside of the cabin, taking down the long narrow shutters that blended into the building perfectly and opening the water flow from a small spring to be available in the house. From the inside the windows could be slid open as shooting portals. The weapons hidden here were brought out and set up around the rooms, upstairs and down.

There was not much more they could do to prepare. Halya started making some sandwiches for their lunch. Everyone would have to eat, no matter what.

Simon went outside and didn't return for quite a while. When he did, he brought the scruffy little rooster and a couple of hens in the pet carrier.

"I just couldn't let this little guy give them away by crowing at the wrong time and becoming some jerks' dinner," he told them. "It sounds like they are camping up the hill near the store and foraging around the area."

They heard a muffled explosion. James and Simon smiled and explained someone had tried dismantling one of their booby-trapped houses. Another explosion was heard a bit farther away. Yes, there went another one of their own bombs.

Gabe found a radio under the counter in the kitchen. It was a HAM radio and he did not know how to use it. James was more familiar with them, so started figuring out the power source and set up. It had a small solar panel hooked to an old battery under the sink. He put the solar panel in the window and after a few minutes, the light came on, on the radio.

After fiddling with it a while, he picked up someone near Tok and gave them the information about the 'Peacekeepers' heading toward Fairbanks on the Elliott. It took a long roundabout way to do it, but finally the man returned to James and let him know the Militia in Fairbanks now had the message and would be heading out to intercept and make a warm welcome for them. Thanks were sent.

James wanted to do a little reconnaissance, so left a bit later. He went by the shop and milked the cow, fed the calf and chickens that were left in the shop and then went on up the hill to see what was happening.

The camp was larger than he expected. Evidently quite a few were injured from the explosions they had triggered at the homes they were planning on entering. The wounded were being cared for near the edge of camp. James wished he had the rocket launcher, he could take care of a lot of them right now, although there were too many for him to make it out alive, if he tried. After thinking it over better, he figured he was better off not having the rocket launcher.

He was walking in the edge of the woods, following the road north a bit to cut down over the hill back to the cabin when he heard the sound of a motor coming. He stepped off deeper into the brush where he had a good view north.

The old pickup headed slowly toward him had seen better days but was still chugging along. He took a chance and stepped out where they could see him. The pickup stopped quite a ways back and someone got out on the passenger side. James figured he was in someone's sights on the driver's side.

He leaned his weapon against his leg and stood with his hands open, away from his body. The person walking toward him was slow but more from age and old injuries than from being careful.

"Rich? Is that you and Travis?" he asked.

Rich turned and motioned toward the truck and it eased forward. Then Travis stepped out.

"You guys almost ran right into the middle of a large camp full of the 'Peacekeepers set up down near the old store," James told them.

"Well, dang. We were told this road was clear all the way to town and we wanted to go see how some friends are doing and maybe pick up some supplies, James. How is the folks that all used to live around here?" Travis asked.

"If you want to pull the pickup off the road and we can hide it a bit, then do a bit of hiking if you want, you can come see for yourselves," James told them. "Dinner should be ready pretty soon."

Travis backed up until he found an area where he might be able to get back on the road later, and pulled the truck off into the trees. They cut some branches and used an old brown tarp in the back of the truck and covered making it harder to find. Travis took the rotor off and pocketed it after disconnecting and placing the battery in the bushes. The old truck didn't have a key and he only used a push button to start it with, on the dash, with a shut off switch.

They walked a bit farther up the road and then cut down over the hill to find the cabin. About halfway there, Travis asked if they were going to Jimmie's old cabin and James told him he thought it was. Travis knew exactly where it was, so they didn't have to stumble around trying to find it from this direction.

When James tapped out their code on the door, Lynn opened it and was enveloped in a giant hug from Travis.

"I was afraid you wouldn't believe me and go on into town, girl. So glad to see you're still here."

The little squeak from her middle made him jump back. When she pulled the light cover away from Aurora, the baby looked up at him and then grinned her biggest grin, showing a new tooth.

Travis stared at her in amazement. Then Rich stepped over to see what Travis was looking at.

"Aww, looky here, a little new Alaskan."

Halya stepped in to say that dinner was ready and Joseph was waving his arms around to make sure everyone was paying attention. He loved meal time.

"Hey Guys, meet Joseph and Aurora. Our two newest residents," Halya said. "Come grab a plate or these two will beat you to it."

During dinner, Travis and Rich were brought up to date on the local happenings and they had some tales to tell also.

Travis did a few radio broadcasts, then he and Rich went out hunting and when they returned, the camp had been overrun by invaders and everyone was gone. They did manage to put enough of the radio back together to hear others broadcasting but were unable to send out.

Gabe showed them the small old set up in the cabin and they started fiddling with it. Soon they had a broadcast coming in loud and clear.

Everyone was warned of several large groups of the invaders that had parachuted in farther north and were making their way south even now. Simon muttered they were already here.

Very early the next morning, they heard sounds of combat up along the road. They considered going up to lend a hand then thought better of it in case someone thought they were part of the enemy. They did patrol around their area and James made it in to milk, feed and water the livestock. There was a lookout at all times in the upstairs room looking all directions from the cabin.

Travis was on watch when he saw sign of a large body of men coming down the hill from up the direction the fighting had been. They wore blue helmets. Gabe and Simon set up the rocket launcher and rockets and started lobbing them into the middle of the advancing group. Lynn had the small machine gun over under the trees just to the north of the group and opened fire as the Militia that was following them caught up from behind.

James came in from the east with the grenade launcher and Rich and Travis opened fire from the upstairs post when anyone came in range. Halya tried to keep the babies from panicking too much, but the noise had them both crying. All she could do was cuddle them and sing to them.

It was over as fast as it has started. The Militia members looking over the unexpected help with a leery eye. When Lynn stepped out and they saw they had a woman on their side, then Halya came out with the two teary eyed babies, they gave a ragged cheer. Their homes and families were what they were fighting for.

The Leader of the Militia group shook hands with Gabe when he set the rocket launcher down.

"Now that isn't something every household has laying around. Sure glad you folks were here, we would have been chasing these galoots all over the hills and they have a habit of setting bombs along their trails just for the fun of it."

"We got it from one of their vehicles last summer, when all this first started. We picked up the rest of the stuff the same way. They are very careless. It sounded like they blew some of themselves up last night with a couple of their own bombs." Gabe told him.

"Couldn't have happened to nicer folk," the man replied.

"Does anyone know how any of these groups are still out and about?" Travis asked him. "We would like to go home since it looks like we can't exactly just go on to town right now."

"Actually, if you still want to go to town and have the means, I would like to hire you to haul some of my wounded in and my reports need turned in. I would rather just keep looking for more, farther along the road, if you would, please?" the Leader told Travis.

Rich and Travis went back up the hill with the Leader and most of his group as the rest were digging trenches to bury the remains littering the ground. They would camp up near the road and leave the next morning.

Gabe and Halya wanted to return home today. Lynn thought they should keep their homes secret, even from these people. She was not very trusting of everyone's intent. James agreed with Lynn that it would be best to keep their homes secret, at least a while longer. He would continue caring for the animals.

Chapter 22

During the night, Lynn woke up to the sound of someone trying to open the door quietly from outside. No one had shown any of the newcomers how to open the hidden catch. Her first thought was maybe Travis or Rich were back. But then she remembered that they already knew about this place and the ways to open all the doors.

She carefully dressed and slid her handgun out of its holster as she made her way quietly to the other door. She eased outside and came around the building behind the scruffy looking fellow trying to jimmy the door open. She looked around the area to make sure he was alone, then smacked him in the head with the butt of her pistol.

When he came to, he was tied to a chair quite firmly and a strip of tape covered his mouth. A cloth was over his eyes so he couldn't see, either. Someone walked into the room and he mumbled behind the tape. No one touched him, no one said a word. Then all was quiet again.

Lynn went back to bed, there was still plenty of hours she could be sleeping and no reason to wake everyone up just because someone wanted to break into their current home.

Then she overslept as Aurora was sleeping through the night and was only playing quietly in her own small bed fashioned from a few boards and pillows. She noticed Lynn was awake and started babbling to her. Lynn smiled back at her and tugged her into her bed for morning nursing. Then she sat her on the little bucket in their room. She had started this from a very early age and Aurora seldom had wet diapers.

When they finally made it downstairs, she abruptly remembered the prisoner as he was still tied, taped and blindfolded in the chair. No one paid any attention to him and it was driving him up the wall. Lynn got some looks and pointed fingers from her to the prisoner, she nodded yes and went on into the kitchen.

She got a drink of water and sat Aurora down in the playpen they had fashioned from some poles for the little ones to keep them out of the way. She handed both babies pieces of jerky which they loved for their new teeth trying to emerge and walked back into the living room.

When she got close to the prisoner, she whispered beside his head, "So, you think you were going to get lucky, breaking in here? Maybe make yourself a new home here? Or were you just so tired you were looking for a place to sleep?"

When she mentioned a place to sleep he vigorously nodded his head in agreement.

"You didn't get the hint yesterday that we really don't take kindly to uninvited guests? We can always dig another trench out by the river for just one more irritating party crasher."

The man cringed back from her and was trying to speak around the tape. She helped him out by ripping it off.

He started cursing and she smacked him across the mouth, rather lightly, and said, "Children. There are small children here and they do not need to hear those kind of words. If you want to speak, you speak politely. Understand?"

As she turned away, he muttered "Bitch," under his breath and she smacked his mouth very hard.

"So, you don't think you can just disappear and join the ones sleeping near the river? I wouldn't test my patience much more if I were you," she told him.

She removed the cloth over his eyes and he blinked several times to focus them. He looked around as though he thought he might find some sympathy for his plight somewhere in the room. Halya was the only other person he saw as the men were all outside, deciding just what should be done. James came back with some eggs and the fresh milk. When he came in the back door in the kitchen, he peeked in to see what the women were doing and almost yelped when he saw Halya approaching the man with a wicked looking knife in her hand as though she knew exactly how to use it.

He stepped back out and asked Gabe what the ladies were going to do to the man.

"I'm not sure, but I think they are actually going to scare him half to death, then turn him over to the Leader of the Militia. We think he deserted last night."

"Well, I think they have already scared him half to death. Just watching them a couple of minutes scared me."

"I don't think it would be a good thing to make either one of them really mad at a person," Gabe told him.

"No kidding. Any time I think I am strong, I just think of what those ladies have put up with and feel a bit wimpy. They are really something." James answered.

"Shall we see if they are done terrorizing him and ready to let us return him to his camp?" Gabe asked.

"Sure, if you think they are really done. I wouldn't want them to take it out on us if they aren't ready yet. Where did they catch him?"

"Lynn caught him trying to break in last night."

"We should have posted a guard. I certainly didn't think we would need one, but guess I was wrong."

When the men stepped into the kitchen, Halya turned to smile at them and then Lynn, did, also.

"Shall we return him or do one of you fellows want to take him back to his outfit?" Lynn asked. "I bet they are going to be really happy to see him back, he is such an upstanding trustworthy individual."

"We better get a move on or they will have already left without him," Gabe told her.

They left the man's hands tied and a short length of rope kept him from thinking he could outrun any of them. Soon they were on their way back up the hill. James and Gabe escorted him to camp as they were getting ready to move out.

The Leader came over to meet them and snorted when he saw the captive. "So, Harkens, you decide to go out on your own last night? You were supposed to be on guard duty. You are lucky they returned you alive so you could receive your punishment from me. Fall in between Geordie and Fowler. They will keep an eye on you."

"But I didn't get any breakfast or even a latrine break. I need some water."

"Should have thought of all those things before you made a nuisance of yourself. Now get over there and get moving."

They watched him trudge over to his position and the men started out heading north.

"Just what happened to him? He looks a bit well used."

"Our ladies caught him and gave him a sneaks' welcome. He is lucky he wasn't wearing a blue helmet or dressed in one of their uniforms. He was trying to break into the cabin last night."

"Well, maybe he will spread the word that these ladies don't take kindly to uninvited visitors."

"They did stress that point."

"Several of the men were impressed by the ladies yesterday. This will make them even better thought of."

"One is from Afghanistan, the other one served there, so neither one is a shrinking violet and they both know how to take care of themselves." Gabe told him.

"Alrighty then, I will pass the word and let them all know not to mess with any of the ladies along this road, they are tougher than they look."

"You can bet that any you find alive out here are very tough ladies and to be handled with care. There are no shrinking violets out here alive."

"Actually, Harkens was considered something of a tough, so the fact a lady caught him and kept him prisoner should give her reputation an even bigger boost. Of course he might try for revenge."

"Not unless he has a death wish. Either one of those ladies will be happy to oblige him, if that is the case."

The Leader laughed and moved on out with his men. They were going to set up patrols along the road system but most of Alaska doesn't have roads, so there was still a lot of country left unattended.

The Leader had told them yesterday that Canada offered planes to fly patrols over more of the State and it was being considered if they could take a local along to point out areas likely to be used by invaders.

***

Canada had made it clear that they would not tolerate any interference from the UN or the President. They had done quite enough already. If the State of Alaska was to be considered undesirable as a State, it should be granted its freedom or allowed to decide its future for itself. Canada would back its decision. The United Kingdom agreed and then several other countries put in their two cents worth on the side of Alaska.

The Secretary of the UN was placed under protective custody, so was the President. A general housekeeping sweep was made throughout the agencies and some alphabet agencies were disbanded or placed on permanent leave. People in positions of power were asked to take an oath of allegiance to the United States of America. Term limits were arbitrarily put in place for everyone serving in Congress. Any raises in pay had to be voted on by the voters on the ballot during Presidential elections. No favoritism on Laws passed, they applied to everyone including the ones passing them. Political correctness was a thing of the past. If someone was too delicate to handle reality, they had to quit being a whiney entitlement oriented wussy and grow up.

There were a few riots. It was no fun rioting when the shop owners were armed and defended their property, so that didn't last too long. Mexico was fast having to defend their own Border as the flow of illegal aliens was now headed that direction. The free ride was over.

Back in Alaska, things were going much better. The Governor was trying to reclaim his Governorship. Everyone told him to return to Mexico. He was not wanted. Then they found copies of the papers exchanged with Washington DC before the invasion began and then everyone was busy wanting him to come back and face charges. He decided he liked Mexico. They kicked him out.

The final mop up of invaders cleared the way for Lynn to move back to her house. She was angry all over again when she found that one of the explosions they had heard was her house when the invaders tried to remove the bomb. The main part of the house was not damaged, but she would have a lot of repairs to do. She would have to wait until freeze up to drive her plow truck on out down the valley from where it was parked. Gabe and Halya asked her to stay the winter in her little house down there, if she wanted to. They enjoyed her company and they didn't have to all be right in each other's way. They asked James and Simon to stay, also. It was talked over a lot.

The gardens planted everywhere were all producing and the greenhouse was a major success. The chickens were thriving and so was the cow and calf. They were cutting hay all along the main roadway and along each driveway and yard. There would still be a possibility of shortages in town this coming winter. The details were still sketchy about resuming commerce.

After much discussion, they all decided to just stay put for the winter. It might be safer until everything was worked out and they already knew they all worked well as a unit. It would be hard to start trying to each gather enough food separately to make the winter on. Dividing up what they had done as a group would not yield enough even though it would be plenty if they stayed together.

James and Simon said they still didn't know if they even had a home to return to, so one afternoon, everyone piled into Lynn's pickup and drove up the road to find out just what might be left at their place.

As they drove up the road to his home, it did not look good. There were broken down military vehicles along his drive and signs of burned out tents and shelters as they drove along. There were no buildings left standing. It was a depressing sight. Neither man even wanted to get out. Lynn had her old camera with her and snapped several pictures.

She wondered if they could file for damages to their property to the UN, since it was responsible. They could try.

They turned around and went home. All of them considered the little underground houses down in the valley as home now. It was warm and inviting and they were all happy there.

They started cutting firewood in earnest along with all the hay they were cutting and gathering. The large seed heads on some types of wild grasses were being cut also. They would be great for the chickens. Buckets of gravel were stockpiled in the garage for not only cat litter but for chicken grit.

They were going to do well this winter. They were ready.

www.ingramcontent.com/pod-product-compliance
Lightning Source LLC
Chambersburg PA
CBHW060637260626
47161CB00008B/2908